Nine Pills

Jonny Halfhead

Copyright © 2018 Jonny Halfhead

All rights reserved.

ISBN-13: 9781728624273

For Helen

CONTENTS

1	The End	1
2	A Wedding	6
3	Not Just A Headache	12
4	Possessed	14
5	Building Up	20
6	Pagan Celebration	22
7	A Day's Worth	33
8	The Coach To Hell	35
9	Overdose	46
10	Public Humiliation	48
11	No Return	57
12	Here We Go Again	59
13	No Return	68
14	The Cure	70
15	Ouroborus	81
16	A New Chapter	83
17	Disintegration	98
18	Freedom	100
19	And Finally	103
20	Stupid, Stupid, Stupid	106
21	Epilogue	112

1 THE END

I can feel the bitter cold breaking up through the thinly carpeted floor. The stains in the bedraggled carpet reveal the full truth of this rooms numerous residencies. Below the cheap weave, there lies a thin plastic veneer above an even thinner sheet of metal and then the outside world. Sitting on the cold floor, I can sense the winter air swirling around the open cavern underneath the floor. How in the name of god and in a civilised society, can a static holiday caravan be passed off as a winter's place of residence, in the middle of northern England?

Above the sound of the freezing, howling wind passing through the underneath of the floor, is the hum and crackle of the record about to start playing on the turntable. I should be able to smell the fatty and fusty odours emanating from this wretched excuse for a carpet, except I have become accustomed to its stench after only a couple of months.

The landlord called the room "Furnished". It's a very basic excuse for the term. I wonder what the caravan must have originally looked like when it was built. It probably had a fancy interior, built in cupboards, clever tables that turned into beds, that kind of thing. I wonder if in some distant past, families went on holiday and stayed in this caravan, lit up with happiness, laughter and expectation. Those days are long gone. Looking around the room, the built in furniture has all gone. There is a single, stained cupboard with a sink on it, a battered standalone electric cooker, a very small fold away dinner table and one single sofa chair. Hardly the décor of a modern "Furnished" palace.

Why would someone rip out all those fitted furniture pieces, I wonder? Spite? It's 1991 and the £35 rent per week obviously doesn't cover such luxuries as comfortable furniture. Furniture would help keep the room warm. There's an electric fire to my left and it is the only source of heat in the whole caravan and it beats out heat by the bar full. Or it would if the caravan wasn't so cold that only if you physically sit on the fire can you feel the heat coming off it. I can hear the electric meter spinning furiously and clunking another 50 pence piece through as the hungry machine feeds of my reluctance to live just that little bit longer. Everyone knows that electricity isn't cheap, but the canny landlord has a sneaky trick up his sleeve, as the meter does not belong to the energy company, but owned by the clever landlord who also makes extra from every neutron passing through the electric feed cable.

The record starts to play a few quiet notes. That warm hum of a record player crackling and rolling it's way to those first notes is always comforting, even when you know all hell could be about to break loose through the needle.

I love this album. When art reflects life, such a close

connection is made and this album has such a close connection to me. Even before the music starts, I know that I am in the presence of an old familiar friend that shares every pain I am feeling.

I don't want to be disturbed. I know full well I'm wallowing in self-pity, but then I am in my own home and why the hell not for once shouldn't I think about myself. I seem to have spent a lifetime being bothered about either what other people think or wondering if I'm upsetting other people and look where that has got me, sinking here in pathetic misery. Well I love my misery. Its darkness and self-loathing along with the music currently playing is keeping me warm against the impossible cold.

On the floor in front of me, I'm placing in a precise and neat line, rows of paracetamol, all white, clean and perfect. They are the angels that will be my salvation, my release. To my right I have a pint glass of water. I was going to drink a nice can of bitter, but I've had planning conversations before.

My Cousin Joseph and I used to talk openly and romantically about the best way to finish one's life. His preferred imagined method was to cut his wrist in a bowl of warm water. He had read how the warm water encourages the blood to flow quickly and freely from the open wound. We both speculated how almost orgasmic the feeling must be to let your own blood pour and flow over your own body, how the warmth must envelop like a comforting blanket and how each pump of your heart would slow as your head started to spin and everything would fade into an almost drunken, euphoric state. All I could ever think about was the mess it would leave behind for others to clear up, not a romantic vision at all.

No, I am going to leave the least amount of mess I can.

It may be a long time before anyone finds me. Hopefully it will just be the landlord. Only three people know I'm here and only one might actually take the time to check up on me and that could take months. Up on the flaky painted wall in front of me are pinned several sheets of roughly scribbled poems I've written over the past couple of months. I wonder if they be my final words? They aren't meant to be and I have no intention of leaving anything in the way of an epitaph. No-one cares what my feelings are when I breathe, certainly no-one will care any greater when I don't. They won't likely mean much to anyone else either as they are the blunt, spluttered feverings of a darkened and confused mind.

The whole bottle of pills are lined up in two lines before me, exact and accurately measured with equal spacing on the record sleeve cover. I will take my time, savour the moment, and wallow in my pity without a care for anyone else. What a relief.

The album lasts an hour, I can take that long to eat the pills one at a time, cry my last tears, sink my heart further and further down into the cold carpet pile. How many pills will it take? I've read the instructions on the bottle. It reads to take two every four hour period and a big notice that says don't exceed four in a day. That's my target to exceed that number and then sleep, oh that sleep.

Isn't it strange how life slows down sometimes? I try to make it slow down all the time. When bad things happen a moment becomes an age, so when good things happen I try and do the same by slowing everything down and savouring every moment. This is a big moment right here and now for me. I will slow down time, appreciate every breath, every sound, every feeling even if they are wasted experiences. I believe that when I go, that is it, there is nothing else. This was my one and only chance of life. As an unrepentant sinner I will die the eternal death.

Time ... stand still.

The cold under my crossed legs, the heat from the electric bar fire, the warm sound from the speakers, the smells of fusty carpet and the sofa I'm leaning against, the darkening evening room and the single spot lamp lighting the room, the damp air filling my lungs are all encompassing. Through the tears in my eyes, running memories down my cheeks, the music playing in my ears, I take the first tablet.

2 A WEDDING

I love weddings. In the congregation we have so many weddings and funerals. But weddings are amazing. Loads of wonderful food, lots of happy people, and lots of games to play.

What a night it has been. Waltz music is playing over the speakers and people are on the dancefloor dancing away in the dimly lit hall. I'm in the most wonderful embrace, my heart is singing. I am so happy to the point that my heart feels like it will explode with an overabundance of love, beauty and adoration.

The congregation always bring themselves together for weddings. There's a unique smell to them. The food is all homemade which gives it a warm and homely feel to proceedings. After the food has been eaten, it's always been tradition to have the children's games, followed by the grown up games, followed by dancing, always to old time dance hall songs and waltzes. There are no disco's here, oh no. Disco with its thumping, gyrating beat is devil music and has no place at a wedding or that's what I'm told.

NINE PILLS

I didn't care about the music at all. I'm lost in a place like heaven and hoping the experience will never end.

For about two hours, I have been wrapped up in the bosom of a beautiful young lady. My angelic blue eyes and soft perfect face had won over an angel of such empathic power, that I felt that neither of us could resist the pull between us. She is softly spoken, and has me wrapped up in such tenderness and love that I don't want to be anywhere else for the rest of my life.

With my head on her chest, I can feel her soft skin against my cheek. Her perfume filling my nostrils with every deep breath as her breast rises and falls, lifting me slowing up and down like floating on calm waters. I can hear her heart beating and her voice from deep inside her chest as she speaks to friends around her.

One of her hands is gently holding my small fist and her other arm is wrapped around my body holding me on her lap. Every so often the group's conversation would lull and I would look up into those amazing eyes of hers as she would look down and catch my admiring stare. As soon as we catch each other's gaze, a huge wash of emotions wave over me from head to toe and she goes through a huge intake of breath and gently squeezes me in her arms. Every time we do this I want to just cry from an overwhelming sense of love and devotion.

I have never felt anything like this before. The whole intensity and the synchronicity of empathy is just overwhelming. I'm very aware that I am only five years old and shouldn't be feeling like this. I'm also very aware that even at five years old, I'm not allowed to have any close female companionship. Even at five years old my every action is scrutinised. I'm actually shocked that I'm getting away with this, but all worries are irrelevant, I just want to stay here forever. My mum has tried a few times in the evening to get me away by charging me with being demanding, but my saviour just insists on keeping me wrapped up in her blanket of love and affection. My mother has tried several times through the evening to poke fun at me lying there like a baby in this women's arms, but I don't care at all. I know how I feel and eventually my mum went away and left the two of us in peace.

Never once this evening has my empathic partner got fed up, or even stopped holding me close, regardless of other people interrupting us to talk and chat. All the way through the evening, she has been taking moments to look down at me, once again make that eye contact, once again squeeze gently and make that strong connection with me. Every time it happens I want to scream out loud with sheer happiness and joy or just burst into a fit of tears. I don't even know who she is. I'm told she is a long distance family member, but I have never met her before. I'm so lost in the moment that I don't even recall how I was so lucky to have ended up in this perfect scenario. All I can do is prompt that connection as many times as possible, which makes my heart is sing so loudly with rapture.

But I know that an end is coming. A darkness is looming as I am totally powerless to stop time in its tracks. I can already hear people starting to leave the wedding and saying their goodbyes. I know some time very soon it will be my loving angel that will be ripped from me.

I feel lost already, like seeing the pain of an accident

coming towards me before the inevitable impact. I wonder what kind of a cruel existence this is to be given something so pure, wonderful and devastating in its beauty that it has to be taken away from me like I don't deserve it. The frustration in me threatens my resolve to saver every second, to enjoy every minute I have until reality rips my heart out. I'm helpless because I do not have a voice. No matter what I say, apart from my angel and empathic partner, no one will notice I have a voice. I'm five years old, and a five year old has no voice, no opinion and no say in anything.

More people say their farewells and I can feel the oncoming doom. The sadness starts to creep up my body like a black slime threatening to devour me as the reality hits that I will be separated from this glorious moment. My all-encompassing love starts to seem more real with each passing minute. It's not just frightening, it's a real threat of total devastation. I have witnessed something so heavenly that being without it seems like its own death, like a path I do not want to walk back on ever again. What is a life without this beauty and perfection?

Strangely I can feel the same empathic connection with my love. She also seems to be holding on to me tighter, trying to make more connections with me, squeezing me gently and warmly more and more.

But then the inevitable happens and her family start to talk about leaving. My heart bursts open and tears just start to stream down my face. I know I will never feel like this ever again. I try not to make it noticeable, but she has noticed and keeps me hidden and safe for as long as she can. She knows that we have this connection and she is also afraid of it being cut off.

My mum notices that the family are all ready for leaving except for my love, still with me, holding me wrapped up in her arms. So my mother tells me sternly to stand up alone and let the woman go home with her family. As soon as my mum sees my tears, she finds it hysterical and makes jokes about how tired I must be with all the usual demeaning language that gets thrown at a crying five year old.

I feel a real sense of foreboding, like storm clouds looming in the distant sky warning of a darkness to come. I am extremely aware that over the past couple of hours I have experienced something pure and beautiful and it frightens me intensely that I may never have that feeling again. Of course it's also terribly confusing as to what this feeling is. I don't even know who the woman is whose embrace, love, warmth and empathy I have been feeding off. I know that any minute now the bubble will burst and reality will come back at me with an uncontrollable thud. My instincts are to find a way out of the inevitable, to somehow dodge and weave my way through the oncoming crash. I start to ask the questions I should have asked hours ago. Who my loving partner is, where will she go back to, when will I see her again. But all the answers just made the coming darkness even bleaker. She is from a long distance away and the way she was talking, I would likely never see her again.

I am devastated and so very confused. I'm a little five year old charmer in my cute little suit, shirt and tie, big blue eyes and rosy cheeks. I can charm most ladies with my adorable sickly cuteness and I know it. I'm very polite and well-mannered and an all-round dream package really. But I have never created this kind of empathic link with anyone else before. This whole experience is something completely new, pure, perfect and mutual. To see it being lost as quickly as these emotions arrived is unbearable.

I start crying uncontrollably, not in a tantrum way, but in a way of total and utter loss. I have such a deep seated horrible feeling that I will never have this experience again in my life. Through the haze of tears I can see my angel's heart breaking. Because of our connection, I can see it in her face and feel it in our shared empathy.

My mum picks me up and carries me away. Within moments we are separated, my love is walking out the door with the rest of her waiting family and she is gone, my heart taken with her.

3 NOT JUST A HEADACHE

That was the first pure white and perfect pill. With a quick sip of water it goes easily down my throat. This is not just another headache to be cured, this is beauty and perfection being devoured. The music plays onto another song, its vibrations ringing sympathetic resonations on my heart strings.

The memory of my first love creates that further sinking loneliness into the cold damp carpet. The same questions and plea for reasoning still rush through my head. Who was she? What was that feeling and why have I never felt that feeling ever again? How can I not have had such a beautiful connection like that again in 15 years? Why would I want to be in a world where my one true experience of pure love, beauty, empathy and connection comes along at such a young age and then never repeats itself?

I can almost see my breath in the cool air. The electric fire is hardly piercing the cold at all. The evening is darkening, matching the beauty of my mood and the determination I have to carry on walking the short road I have started down. Although different, this is another purity, another perfection and another connection as that felt by my five year old self. It just feels slightly different in the way that many human faces have similar features but all are distinct and unique. As much as I want to feel that pure love again, I know that I never can. I also know that this moment now is also beautiful, dark and pure and will be another lost moment, soon washed away and gone like all the other moments before it.

I want to enjoy this moment, this purity of intent. The white tablets in perfect symmetrical lines in front of me remind me of the path I am on and I obey their call and pick out another and throw it in my mouth.

4 POSSESSED

I'm so frightened. Why does this keep on happening to me? I have nothing to hang on to as I'm thrown about at a thousand miles an hour, uncontrollably, round and round. In my hand I can feel that strange sensation I always feel when these weird experiences happen, a piece of grit between my forefinger and thumb that has the weight and mass of a planet. Everything is surreal, like a super coloured dream. I'm not asleep and yet I'm hovering at the top of the staircase, a couple of feet off the floor. And yet instead of just the staircase stretching down in front of me, there is a huge whirlpool of gases and planets and stars that have picked me up and is hurtling me around with the rest of the galaxy in miniature. It is all too real to be a dream. It's the same as every other time it has happened. I know why I'm here, it's because I wasn't strong enough to fight it off just a couple of hours ago.

My shouting and screaming with horror wakes up my mum and she comes running out of her bedroom. I cannot believe she is asking me what is wrong even though she must see the absolute panic and horror in my face. My mum being there somehow breaks the illusion down, although not immediately. The spinning galaxy starts to slow down and slowly I am lowered gently back to the floor.

I lay on the floor in my mother's arms soaking with sweat and thoroughly exhausted from my exertions. I still have the fear, like battery acid running through me, I know at any time it could kick off again. I can still feel the shadow of that piece of grit between my forefinger and thumb and I try not to let my two fingers meet in case it starts the whole process off again.

This isn't the first time this has happened. My mother has had several crackpot theories of her own as to what it is that keeps happening to me. She thinks she knows what the doctors do not
.
I've had other sleepwalking problems for some time. It's a problem that has always unnerved me. Some evenings my mum would have people visit for dinner. In the early evening, I and my siblings would go to bed and the guests would stay chatting into the evening. There were a few instances where an hour or so later I would be walking downstairs in my pyjamas, sitting in the living room wide awake and having full interactive conversations with my mum and her guests. The problem is, I'm getting to that age where I don't want my mum to know everything I do and think. I'm a young teenager and I have thoughts that aren't always as pure as they are supposed to be and I know what my mum is like, she will interrogate me on one of those occasions. My mother believes that all males are filthy, disgusting, sex crazed creatures that need to be controlled by gods laws and the strict chastity of those around them in order to keep everyone sin free.

My mother actually has worry on her face. I can see the helplessness in her eyes and the panic running through her. That should be a comfort to me, except for prior experience of how these things usually work out. The first time I had these hallucinations, my mother threw out all her ABBA vinyl records. She decided that because ABBA where such a wife swapping, immoral set of people when those records were made, that somehow through that sin and debauchery the devil had infiltrated the house and therefore me through those records. I was possessed by a demon. So my mother didn't just throw out all her ABBA records, but made sure that she also smashed them into pieces, just in case someone else rummaged through our dustbin and decided they would have the records for themselves and therefore like a disease, would pick up the evil demons onto themselves unknowingly. I never really understood my mum's logic with any of her thinking. Those records had been in the family for years. The news of ABBA's divorces was years ago, why the demons waited many years to come out of the records, I have no idea. I also couldn't understand why demons would choose such a random set of hallucinations to make mischief with, do they really have nothing better to do?

The next time I had a full blown hallucination episode, my mother continued to look around the whole house and try and find any tainted belongings that once again had brought in the devils influence from outside. What was different that second time was having the hallucinations in the middle of the day and in the presence of my grandad. He told my mother to take me to the doctors. Unfortunately the doctors did a couple of tests and deAmyd they had no clue what was happening to me. I wasn't on any medication and they took a blood test that didn't reveal anything. That just made my mum more determined that it was demons at work.

After running around the whole house searching, my mum centred on a large teddy bear that I had had since I was a baby. It was one of two very large teddy bears I owned, one of which my parents bought for me as a baby, the other one was apparently found and rescued from somewhere about the same time. Because that second teddy bear's origins years ago were not known, my mother took it as a likely candidate for a long dormant demon influence that for some reason had suddenly awakened and decided to play tricks on me. I didn't understand the argument at all, to me it seemed like a wild stab in the dark really.

Of course my mum couldn't just stuff it into the dustbin. The teddy bear had to be disposed of completely so that no other poor unsuspecting child could be struck down by the evil demon that obviously lay within. The teddy bear got torn limb from limb and its stuffing removed and tied up in a separate bag and put into a different dustbin to the rest of the teddy bear. I was a little distraught, after all it that was one of my childhood companions, but my sister took it worse. Even though she is a couple of years younger than me and is also too old for a teddy bear, my sister totally blamed me for our old cherished stuffed friend being quartered and sentenced to a horrific death. Everything was always my fault in my sister's eyes, even though the decision to destroy the teddy bear had nothing to do with me, it was purely my fault that it got disposed of in such a horrific way.

Needless to say, after the dismemberment of my old stuffed friend, the demons hadn't been disposed of along with the teddy bears separated innards. I soon had more sessions of hallucinations. My mum even brought in an "Elder", one of the congregations priests, to put a blessing on the house. That didn't work either.

The current incident was no different. My mum started talking about what could be left in the house still drawing this demonic influence into me. I can still feel the huge weight between my forefinger and thumb that threatens to kick the whole show off again, but I managed to relax and bring myself away from the abyss. It's the middle of the night and the noisy commotion has awoke both my sister and my little brother.

The panic is subsiding and the sweating diminishes. I can still strongly feel the fear that it could easily kick off again though. I hold the palms of my hands out so that my fingers stretch out, if I stop my finger and thumb touching maybe I can keep the madness at bay.

I feel like such an idiot. I know I'm not making any of it up, but I also know that no-one else can see the things I was seeing. Thankfully my mum believes that something is happening to me, my sister obviously thinks I'm faking the whole scenario up to get attention. I don't do anything to get attention, I really don't want attention, in fact most of the time I want people to just ignore me and go away.

I slowly get to my feet and my mum guides me downstairs and into the living room. My mum asks my brother to get my bed cushion and duvet and to bring them into the living room. With a rare care and attention, my mum sets up the settee for me to sleep on for the night and sets up a couple of lamps to keep the room lit. I'm not comfortable with this attention, it's nice in some ways and yet in other ways it's unnerving. I don't get much attention from my mum and when I do it's nearly always negative. I'm always in trouble, always wrong and my sister has very clever methods of manipulating my mum against me. This attention just makes trouble all the more likely.

The cushion and duvet are set up on the settee and I'm instructed to get under the duvet and try and settle and get some sleep. My sister and brother are sent to bed and my mum sits with me as the room quietens and returns back to its midnight silence.

As my mother sits next to me and the normality is resumed, my mum looks around the room and becomes transfixed with the ceiling.

"That light fixing hanging from the ceiling, we didn't buy that we got it from somewhere". Oh no here we go again.

"It's three pronged, I think that's a trinity light, probably from a catholic household. As Jehovah's witnesses we don't believe in the trinity, it is a false teaching. That light must be bringing a demon influence into the house. I'll get grandad to take it down and throw it in the dustbin tomorrow".

5 BUILDING UP

Two pills down. I'm not going to have a headache this evening at least. Maybe after taking a couple more I might actually not feel the cold anymore. I've never taken more than two paracetamols in one go in my whole life. I don't usually take pills at all. Even if I'm ill, sleep is usually my cure for nearly everything.

I'm starting to feel such a sense of peace and relaxation, even through the tears flooding down my face. More than anything else I feel a sense of pity. If I could detach, hover over and watch myself, I would pity the poor creature in this room. In a world that is selfish, greedy, political, blind and obsessed, I have always tried so hard to be kind, caring and loving to everyone. I have always had a strong belief in bettering myself, that as a person I can always be improved upon and can always strive for a greater personality, to be a warmer person. Yet in a world as cold as the wind blowing around this caravan, I'm not even noticed. I can't make an impact on my own life, no matter anyone else's. Even when I try to reach out and help people, that help is either rebuffed or taken without a thought of repayment back into the universe. I feel so out of balance with everyone else on the planet. I can only grab snippets of solace from other people's art, like the music now playing through my heart from the turntable.

This is now it, this is the most paracetamols I ever taken in one go. Number three

6 PAGAN CELEBRATION

The rain is running down the side windows of the car. It's cold again. My breath steams up the window every time I exhale. The rain just doesn't seem to be letting up at all and reflects the mood in the car. My heart is sinking, I can't believe this is happening. I look at my sister. She has a very smug face on her like she has just won the big prize of the day. I look over to my brother who is still sniffling from crying for the last half hour. He looks at me and I can see the look on his face, he knows that he has been deceived. I really feel for my little brother, he always gets caught up and used by my sister whenever there is a sibling battle to be won, he always gets used then spat out.

The three of us restlessly squirm about on the car seats. It's so cold and the rain playing rhythms on the roof make it seem even colder and more miserable. The car is parked on a housing estate north of Chesterfield. We have never been here before and I have no idea exactly where we are. The houses we are parked outside of are typical, semi-detached concrete counsel estate homes, the same as everywhere around Chesterfield.

I'm very curious as to where we are, although I've been told not to question. Somewhere inside one of those houses is my dad. The guy is practically a stranger, but I get the feeling I'm supposed to know him. Other people at school all know their dads, the kids in the congregation all know their dads too, but all their dads live at home with them. I can't help being curious as to who he is. I do see him from time to time, but I never really know what to say to him. Every time I do meet him it's very awkward as well as I am not allowed to be myself when with him.

We wait in the car, my brother folding his arms looking totally fed up, my sister sat all prim and proper in the front passenger seat like the cat that got the milk. I'm in a foul mood and just feel empty, hollow and worthless. I now know with certainty that I do not have a voice at all, I do not exist.

Just moments ago, my mum ran out of the car in the pouring rain and down one of the garden paths with a full plastic bag full of goodies. I sit with my face to the window hoping that by some small miracle she will re-appear with that same plastic bag, still full of boxes.

I know there is practically no hope of that happening, but I still keep wiping the mist from my breath off the window and continue to stare through it, praying for something to go my way for a change.

My dad left home when I was about seven years old. It was quite unusual then to just have one parent. I didn't understand why it happened and I still don't really know now, except for the fact that my mum constantly tells me how evil he is, like teddy bears, ABBA records and light fittings are evil I suppose. Yes, I'm starting to get a bit cocky, time is making me realise that there are a lot of things around me that just don't add up.

I hadn't seen anything of my dad for a number of years, when out of the blue my sister and I are were being dragged to a court building and being told to say some strange things. It turns out that my dad went to court to try and get permission to see his three children. My mother and Grandmother then conspired to try and stop this from happening at every possible opportunity. Of course it got to court and during proceedings the judge decided that he actually wanted to talk to my sister and I to actually find out what we wanted.

To tell the truth, I didn't care that much. I barely remembered my dad by that time, the majority of my self aware years were spent without him. I had a few fading memories of him, but then I also had several years of both my mum and grandparents telling me how awful, evil and twisted he was. He became like a sort of Darth Vader figure. A shadowy family figure that was always at the deepest parts of hidden unspoken conversation, except for almost a cursed spattering when mentioned out loud.

My sister and I where asked to talk to the Judge in his chambers alone where he would ask us some questions regarding our father. Although my mum and grandmother promised the courts they would not spend time preparing us, prepare us they did. Both spent a lot of time with my sister and I explaining why my dad was an evil anti-christ, a disfellowshipped man. In the Jehovah's Witnesses religion, any person sinning against the church is excommunicated and no-one, even family, are allowed to look at them, talk to them or have anything to do with them until they repent and go back to the church. Some years ago my dad apparently committed adultery against my mum and the church and so was disfellowshipped or excommunicated from the church. The religion was clear about how everyone is to act towards him.

So before we went to see the judge, my mum and grandmother laid it down thick about how much we will be sinning if we agreed to see my dad and made it clear how god would be angry with us if we agreed to see him. They both painted a picture of how the devil would manipulate the judge to trick and deceive us into agreeing to see my dad. By the time it came to meeting the judge, I was absolutely terrified.

I remember sitting outside the judge's room with my sister, wondering what I was going to be subjected to once inside. Then just before being called in to see the judge, my mum, a look of sudden panic in her eyes, told me that more than anything, I needed to just tell the truth. That was about the only thing that did made sense to me. Disfellowshipping, even as a youngster, never made sense to me. How can we and god be loving if we are then asked to act without love and with cruelty towards another person? For me it never had any logic to it. Growing up I saw how disfellowshipped people were treated and even those that repented and returned where still always treated differently and with mistrust for the rest of their lives.

Someone at the court came to us and asked my sister and I to follow them into a room. Inside an old dark wood room, looking just like the old court rooms on TV, a greyed haired man sat waiting for us. He said hello and introduced himself and after just a couple of moments, he made us totally at ease. The judge told us that all that mattered was that we just told the truth. He cleverly steered clear of our beliefs and just asked us truthfully what we thought of our father and what we thought of meeting him. My sister in her usual way just spouted the rehearsed lines and view, I however told the truth, that I didn't know him anymore and that I didn't have an opinion either way as I had no feelings for someone who was basically a stranger.

When we came out of the judge's room, my sister took great pleasure in telling my mum how bad I had been. What a surprise, I was in trouble. I thought I had been truthful and honest, which to my thinking could never be wrong.

Out of those court proceedings came the legal right for my dad to meet us one day a month and take us out for the day. The first time my dad turned up on an arranged Saturday and parked outside our house, my mum told us we didn't have to go out and meet him and reminded us how sinful it was to talk to someone who was disfellowshipped. So we stayed in the house and peeked out the window and watched him sit, humiliated in the car in front of our house. He parked there for about an hour, then when none of us looked to be making an appearance he drove off.

After that first visit, he must have complained back to the court as on his second visit my mum changed tack with us. Instead of encouraging us to ignore him, my mum and grandmother told my sister and I to call him by his first name "Ben".

That was an unbelievable thing to ask of us. It crossed a line in my young and malleable conscience. It had been drilled into me for years, never to call a grown up by a first name as it was extremely rude and ignorant. We were always told to use Mister, Miss or if the person was more friendly and known then Uncle or Aunt. No grown-ups were ever addressed by their first name and if as a child I did, I was punished for it. Even when neighbours insisted we call them by their first name, we were strictly not allowed, as to do so was disrespectful. To have my mum and grandmother, my peers and life tutors, telling me to break that rule and call someone by their first name was for me an act of unprecedented cruelty and humiliation towards the person it was pointed against.

When my dad called that second time, my mum ushered us out the door as she waited in hiding, watching everything we did and listening in. My sister was as pleased as punch to do her mother's bidding and get those sought after brownie points with a loud "Hello Ben!" thrown across the garden like a poisoned spear straight at my dad. Those words made me visibly cringe as I heard them. My sister really didn't have a conscience at all. There was a visible look of shock on my dad's face, but at least we were talking to him.

That's how it went for a few months. My dad would turn up for ritual humiliation and we would all be quite passive about him being there. We never volunteered to get in the car and go anywhere, in fact we rarely ventured off the garden.

By the end of that first year of visits, we weren't even aware of when he was next due and would sometimes miss him because we had gone out to play somewhere.

It was earlier today he turned up at our house and nobody was there. We were all at my grandparents. My mother must have known this was our scheduled day, but she held it with even less importance than we did, even though a court had ruled otherwise. My dad knew where my grandparents lived just around the corner from our house, so on finding an empty house, he must have decided to just chance it and go around to my grandparent's house.

I saw him as he pulled up outside my grandparents' house. "Hello Ben" I said as he wound the car window down. By now I was fully implicated in the naming crime as well. My mother had given me many reasons why my dad wasn't to be respected, the greatest excuse being "he's not your father, a father lives at home and looks after his family". It still didn't sit right though and like having an out of body experience, every time I called him "Ben" I could feel my conscience blunting from the repeated impact.

Despite all the abuse, my dad showed infinite patience. Today he had brought along something special and asked my brother and sister to come out to the car. Once we were all gathered next to the car, my dad produced a plastic bag full of wrapped up presents, one for each off us. Apparently, it was coming up towards Christmas. We had no idea, we had never celebrated Christmas, for us it was just a holiday period away from school.

My dad passed a present to each of us and we politely and excitedly said thank you for each gift we received. The commotion had attracted my mum and grandmother outside who straight away I could tell did not approve. My dad asked us to unwrap the presents while he watched, so we frantically ripped off the wrapping paper. I didn't notice what my brother and sister had I was so transfixed with what my dad had bought me.

To my great shock, it was digital watch. It was the stuff of science fiction. I had only ever seen the odd one or two digital watches ever, they were cutting edge tech. I was blown over by the fact that my dad knew how unbelievable a gift like that was. We never had any money, to own something as amazing as that was beyond my wildest dreams. From the commotion, I could tell that both my sister and brother were just as excited by their presents too.

After an hour of grateful thanks, my dad finally drove off and I was left running around with a proud new digital watch on my wrist looking like the happiest boy on the planet. My mum instructed us all to go inside and sit at my grandmother's dining room table and lay out our presents out on the table. Around the table was my mum, grandmother, my brother, sister and I. I had a horrible feeling that I knew where this was going to go.

We put our presents on the table in front of us as. My grandmother then started to explain why we couldn't accept Christmas presents and why it was wrong to not only to celebrate Christmas, but to encourage others to celebrate it by accepting their gifts. Then my mum talked on at length as to why my dad was trying to use bribery to win us over and why the act of giving his children presents was an immoral and corrupt one. Of course my sister was totally taken in. There was maximum points for her to scored right there. Both my grandmother and my mum said it was a choice they could not make for us, but to let our conscience decide what we should do with our presents. In a very clever way, they both managed to persuade my sister that her conscience argued for wanting to give the gifts back to my dad. I didn't understand that, surely in a case of conscience it would be wise to give the presents to charity or someone else that would benefit greatly from them and thus not hurt anyone by it, that was my argument. So in a vote we were one against one with my poor little brother being the deciding vote on what to do with our Christmas presents.

My sister, mother and grandmother all persuaded my brother to vote their way. I didn't feel I had a right to tell my little brother what his conscience told him. Needless to say he voted to hand the presents back to our father, not really understanding the implications of what he was voting for. I could tell by he didn't understand because he voted with a big smile on his face.

It was only now back in the car with tears running down his face, my brother realises the consequences of his choice.

As soon as the votes were in, my mum was herding all three of us into the car, presents all boxed back up again and stuffed into a plastic bag and hurtling with all pace down the road into Chesterfield.

I knew how it was going to end, this was a life that was becoming so predictable. I had no say in our family at all, mostly because I was male and therefore evil by default. I was never going to own anything of any worth, partly because anything of value was seen in my mother's religious eyes as materialistic, but also because out of the family, without any doubt I was of the least importance. I was my father's son. My sister was her mother's daughter and my little brother was seen as malleable. I was seen as having the devil in me before I spoke even a word.

Still we waited, the rain running down the steamed up car windows. My mother had driven with such delight on her face. I guessed that we were at a house where my dad was likely living. I couldn't understand why it was taking so long for mum to return, she wouldn't be remotely interested in talking, she would just hand the presents over, with some religiously righteous excuse to try and make it as embarrassing and humiliating as possible for my dad.

Through the steamed up windows of the car, I see a figure appearing from behind the house. It's my mum, without the plastic bag of gifts she carried away. My heart sinks as the realisation dawns that I'll never have an amazing digital watch like the one we have just given back. As I wipe the window to see more clearly, I can see my mum walking backwards, nearly tripping over the steps on the path leading from the house back up to where the car is parked. From behind the house comes another figure, a woman, waving her arms, shouting and screaming the kind of obscenities I've only heard before in the school playground.

All three of us in the car scramble to look through the misty windows as our mum comes back to the car shouting abuse back at the women at the house, like some childish sibling fight my sister and I have at home.

Mum gets in the car, flustered, dripping wet through from the rain, visibly shaking and crying her eyes out. For the first time, I really didn't feel sympathetic towards my mum's tears, in fact I partially found it funny in a sort of naughty, secret way. My mother deserved it and had obviously met someone that would stand up to her. My sister asked who the person was shouting and screaming obscenities from outside the house still as my mother fumbled to get the car keys from her pocket and get them into the ignition.

"That's your dad's tart, his floozy"
Wow, my dad has a new partner?

Finally my mum got the keys into the ignition, turned them and got the car fired up and with a panic, shoved it into first gear and revved the car high and sped fast down the street. We didn't drive very far, perhaps only a few miles, with my mum looking around frightened and paranoid looking to see if anyone was following her. Eventually she pulls over and parks up randomly on a street and starts wailing and crying her eyes out. My sister is full of sympathy and cuddles, but I want to have nothing to do with this. To me the whole day's episode had been one big childish tantrum, and while I want to have my own tantrum at having lost such an amazing gift, I really feel like I have lost my mother. It is a child having a temper cry in that front seat, not a role model.

7 A DAY'S WORTH

I still don't feel any different. I have three white pills inside my stomach and I am on the second side of the double vinyl album that is currently playing. I don't have a clue how long these pills will take to start to affect me. They are supposed to be instant relief when you take paracetamol for a headache. So surely all three of these pills are already doing their thing?

All that matters is that this beautiful place I am in doesn't change. As long as I keep the regime true, tidy and systematic, everything will be perfect. I don't want to be conscious when these pills do kick in. I don't want to be in agony and pain. So I will stick to the plan and sleep, a beautiful forever sleep. A nothing.

I don't cry because I am sad, I cry because I am alone. But I am in the only company that truly understands how I feel, except for those words being sung and the beautiful sounds that vibrate through my very soul rom the record on the turntable.

This is pill number four. This is a double dose now and

there is no turning back. With this pill I will be taking a full day's dose and I am on the correct and only truth path I can be on. This is purity, this is beauty, this is perfection.

8 THE COACH TO HELL

The descent is happening so fast. One minute I was in a world of total euphoria and now I am descending into the very pit of hell at lightning speed. How can such a massive high be followed with such tragic reality and low. I'm dying while surrounded in daylight, members of the public and a close friend. In my hand I have a wrapped up lunch that I'm struggling not to squeeze and destroy through sheer frustration and fear.

Thankfully it's been the slowest week of my life. Every minute of it that has passed I have slowed down time purposefully and savoured every remarkable moment. Now it's all over and done and with a crash reality comes smashing back into view. I want to die, right now.

As the coach starts to pull away I fantasize about a sudden and catastrophic accident that gives me a quick and painless end. That would be so satisfying and appropriate, except for taking my friend with me which wouldn't be so clever at all.

Oh no. I've just realised, my close friend is sat next to

me, very likely looking forward to getting home to his family. I have not treated him with much respect at all this last week In fact it's suddenly dawning on me the terrible situation I have forced him into. I have been so wrapped up in my dream week that I completely forgot how my actions may have consequences for the young man sat next to me. There will likely be a reckoning.

I take in a deep breath and I can smell the fabric on the coach. Why do all coaches have such a distinct fusty smell? I can feel the cold through the large window I am leaning against starting to pierce into my shoulder. The cold feels like my heart slowing dying. Outside the world starts to move past me faster and faster as the coach leaves the city and starts the journey home to Chesterfield. I certainly don't want to go back home. Home will have consequence, home will be back to my mixed up family, home will be cold without her there.

It was just over a year ago I met Katie. She was visiting from Cardiff a girl in my local congregation. Every Friday evening I used to go swimming, and that Friday the girl in our congregation and Katie were there too. Katie and I just clicked straight away. I was seventeen and Katie was sixteen and I plucked up the courage to ask if she would write to me once she returned home. That was so sneaky for me. I knew my mother wouldn't approve, she didn't approve of me talking to any females at all.

A couple of weeks later I was delighted to have a letter through from Katie filled with general notes about her home and her life in South Wales and the congregation there. It took a few letters back and forth before my mum started to ask me questions about who I was writing to before she would release the letters to me each week. I had no choice but to be honest, I didn't really know a life other than being honest. "God sees all".

I knew I was walking a tightrope. If my mum had her way, I would never meet a girl because I was not good enough for anyone. I was always a disappointment in everything, there was nothing at all my mother was proud of me with. And because I was a man, I was filthy and wretched and sinful and should be watched at all times and locked up the rest of the time at least in regards to relationships. I love road cycling and I go out in the summer for the entire day without a care of where I am from my mum. And yet, if I wanted to go where there were girls, I had to be watched closely and supervised.

That was just the way of the religion really. No sex before marriage, no homosexuality, no fondling or kissing that might lead to unmentionable fornication. Everyone had to be chaperoned by everyone else at all times. Even masturbation is a deadly curse and a heavy sin that will lead to all sorts of illnesses and diseases. The religion portrays the rest of the world held in a constant state of sexual ecstasy where everyone is at it with everyone else at every opportunity. So my mum always made sure she guarded the rest of the world from me.

Of course it never occurred to me to lie to my mum and about what I was doing or where I was going as I always thought that nothing is hidden from God, I would always be found out.

To my great surprise my mum didn't stop me from writing to Katie, which I was extremely shocked by. This was the first female I could talk to privately, all be it slowly and by post. Still after a couple of months, Katie and I had got letter writing down to fine art. We could manage two letters a week if we replied very quickly. The post took a day, delivery another, read, write and post again on the same day and you could just squeeze two letters into a six day postage week.

As the year progressed I was falling head over heels for the beautiful spirit writing those words back to me. The more we opened up to each other, the more daring we got with our feelings, all be it in still a very naive and innocent way. I would try and sneak the word "love" on the end of the letter, or a single kiss x. Over time the same would be returned, then many kisses, followed by words of love and devotion. By the end of the year, Katie was putting drops of her perfume onto the letters, much to the constant amusement of my mother.

Katie's letters where a ray of light, love, hope and sunshine in the otherwise dark and hopeless world that I lived in.

After nearly a year of letters, Katie's mum invited me to go and stay with them for a week in Cardiff. Immediately I knew there was no chance of that ever happening, my mum would never allow it in a thousand years. But to my total surprise and bemusement she agreed, but only if I took my friend with me as a chaperone.

I had never been allowed to go anywhere on my own before for more than a day even at my age, such was the hold my mother has over me.

I had hopes building up to the week of the visit. The way

my life always seems to pan out meant that I had clear and distinct understanding of the difference between dreams and reality. If anything romantic was to occur from my visit, I promised myself over and over before the visit that I would saviour every single moment, I would slow down time and make sure that I lived every single second and cherished every second.

It was to be Christmas week when I would visit. As a Jehovah's Witness the Christmas week is just another set of bank holidays. We don't celebrate Christmas at all, but everyone is on holiday, which is always advantageous for arranging days out and social events. For the couple of months leading up to the end of the year I was constantly waiting for my mum to suddenly return to her expected default and cancel my trip and not allow me to go. Every day that passed and got nearer without a change of plan was a minor miracle and actually started to make me believe that maybe love was possible boosted by the increasingly romantic worded and perfumed letters that came my way.

Even when I was waiting with my suitcase at the coach station with my friend, I still believed my mum would change her mind at the last minute. But she didn't and I got away and experienced the greatest high of my life.

Sitting staring out the window of the coach, my heart sinking ever and ever deeper, I can at least take pride in doing what I set out to do and saviour every moment of this past week. It has been like a dream that I'm suddenly awaking from. The fact that I've hardly slept all week doesn't help that either, as everything seems surreal.

I was so nervous when we arrived in Cardiff late on that winters night a full week ago. The journey had taken eight hours on the coach and I watched every mile go past wondering with nervous excitement whether all those letters Katie wrote to me were just posturing or whether this girl felt what I felt about the person I thought was on the other end of that friendship. I was fully aware how easy it would be for someone to be totally fake and pretend to be someone else by letter instead of the real person they are, but I thought I was sure that there was no reason to keep a pretence going with such enthusiasm for a whole year if there was not something genuine behind it.

That first encounter, the knock on the front door of the house, was so terrifying. But Katie was beyond wonderful. Within an hour or so of turning up at the door, Katie's parents had introduced themselves, showed us to our rooms and gone to bed for the night, leaving my friend, Katie and myself to our own company. From my world of constant chaperoning, Katie's parents disappearing and leaving her daughter with two strangers was just odd.

That first night was the only night I did not spend with Katie. Each night we all stayed up late not wanting the day to end, until my friend would give up and go to bed and eventually leave Katie and myself alone to our loving explorations and passions. Each night got more erotic and daring until finally one night Katie asked if I would make love to her. That was a moment I had hoped for so much leading up to this week and also had prepared myself for. Instead of letting that passion go that far, I had planned to propose to Katie if the option of sex came up. That was my plan and that is exactly what I did. Instead of make love we promised ourselves to each other that in the next few years we would marry. Basically I devoted the rest of my life to her. The fact she agreed just sent me to heaven. I had a future.

Katie was magnificent. As the week went on our night activities got all the more emotionally involved and passionate and as our passions intensified through the nights we were letting the daytime's public showing of our emotions show. Initially we would play an act in the day, to try and not arouse suspicion with parents and my friend, but as the week progressed it seemed as though we were cheating ourselves and the time we had together to not make the most of every moment we had and at least acknowledge each other, get lost in each other's eyes, or even god forbid hold hands. By the end of the week we were obviously totally in love with each other to anyone that bothered to open their eyes.

At the beginning of the last evening we had together, Katie went into a tantrum and started to cry and push me away. Eventually Katie's mum sat me down with Katie and told me that Katie had been in trouble with the congregation before for having a sexual relationship with another girl. This didn't bother me at all, in fact I just didn't care, to me Katie was beautiful, perfect and amazing and we were going to spend the rest of our lives with each other. Once the air was cleared, everyone left Katie and I alone in her bedroom for the rest of the night.

At the time I thought that a little odd, that Katie's mum left us unchaperoned in Katie's bedroom last thing at night, but I was so wrapped up being with the love of my eternity that any other thoughts of consequence had long since gone. In fact because I refused to have sex with Katie only a couple of nights before, I was so very proud of myself to have enough strength of character to take the longer view rather than the short term satisfaction of having sex that I had my head held high, I was proud. I also had made the most of every second, every moment as I promised to myself that I would and I had been totally unselfish and patient, very considerate and responsive to Katie in all ways that I could. It had been a week of purity, perfection, love and beauty.

Only minutes earlier, I was coming to the end of a week of absolute light and happiness in a lifetime of misery, confusion and darkness. My life was like a train tunnel in reverse. I had gone from miles of dark track into a tunnel of light, only to now come out the other side back into darkness.

A part of me wonders what is going to happen to me now. I had no intention of telling anyone the details of what an amazing week I've had, I also doubt Katie would want to ruin what future we have set up by confessing what we have both done. Katie and I have been in tune all week. I wouldn't want to compromise what we have. I strongly feel that it's nobody else's business anyway and our religion would only make what was pure and beautiful into something filthy and sordid. I know my mother would think the same way for certain.

I find it remarkable that such great contrasts of mood can exist within me and this extreme of light and dark. I really don't want to face up to reality and go back to the pathetic life I have back home. Nothing in my life has compared to this last week. How can I go back to the old world when I have moved on so far and experienced so much? There's an awful feeling that creeps around my head that I will never see Katie again, that no matter what I think I share with her, no matter what we have promised to each other, that there are other forces that will forever keep us apart.

After travelling on the coach for an hour and getting further away from any light that Katie had shared with me and into a greater and greater darkness as the miles past away under the coach, there's a growing sense of dread as to what is waiting for me at home. I don't want to talk to anyone at home, I don't want to look at them, interact with them and most of all I have no interest in putting on the happy face and pretending I'm glad to be back home in that dull black and white existence. I just want to be wrapped up in love for the rest of my life, not constantly having to watch my every move and feeling guilty for breathing and having breath.

There hasn't been much conversation between my friend and I. I can tell he's looking forward to going home and bless him, he's not saying anything about his suspicions of the previous week. This is the Jehovah's Witnesses state we live in. If he suspects any wrongdoing at all he has an obligation to tell the elders about it. His own dad is an elder. The whole unspoken point of him being with me for the last week was to be a chaperone. I sit hoping that he decides to not have an opinion, or to suspect anything by some strange and weird miracle and he just leaves things as they are. He is a good friend, but in the religion, it is supposed to be for love of your brother that a friend tells the authorities in the congregation of anyone's misdemeanours.

In my hand, nearly crushed from the stress of the million things running through my brain, is the last remnant of a life lived briefly in South Wales. Katie's mum had packed the two of us a few sandwiches to eat on the coach on the way home. I had nothing else to show from the last week in my lover's arms except for the memory of total love, warmth and devotion except for a wrapped up snack in tin foil.

I pull the tin foil away from the contents inside, wondering what was going to be in the sandwich. The smell hits me as soon as just a corner of tin foil peels away. It looks like cheese and pickle. I've never had pickle before. Its brown lumpy contents had always been a bit repellent to me and the smell was always so very strong and vinegary. My instinct is to throw it away, but this is the last meagre morsel of evidence of anything at all from the last week. I am not going to turn my nose up at it.

Cautiously, I nibble a corner of the sandwich with hardly any pickle on it. It's perfect. I can't believe that I have never tried pickle before, the combination with the cheese and the thick white bread is just wonderful and it dances on my taste buds. Within moments the sandwich becomes another of the experiences of the past week all wrapped together. New tastes, new experiences with just a little bit of familiarity mixed in, and a finite amount of time before it would all be gone. The sandwich paralleled my inability to let the past week go. I take small, tiny nibbles of my lunch, savouring every small piece and rolling it around in my mouth, maximising the taste extraction before reluctantly swallowing it. Each bite takes me further away until there is little of my sandwich left. I might get to eat another cheese and pickle sandwich in my life, but I know somewhere deep down that eating that same sandwich again is a moment gone and passed.

9 OVERDOSE

The needle rumbles on the exit groove of the record. Side one has finished and the tone arm picks up and returns to its resting place. I still don't feel anything different yet. Now though I move into a different phase. Four pills is a day's dose, now I move into unknown territory.

I get up and turn over the record to get side two playing and drop down to the floor before the music starts up again. The opening bars lift my spirit and tears fill up in my eyes and overflow down my cheek. This really is beautiful. I feel content that in my life I have tried to be beautiful myself, I have tried always to be a better person, a good person. The sadness I feel is the confusion as to why that is not worth anything to anyone out there. If I met anyone with my heart, I would be instantly be in love with them, I would love them completely and without regret. I cannot help but wonder why, in a world of love, and even more importantly from the religious society that I grew up with, why love isn't enough.

This is pill number five. This really is now the end, there cannot be any turning back as this will start to do damage.

The instructions on the pill bottle say so. Now I am walking into a pure depth of beauty and for once it belongs only to me.

The rain continues to hit the window, the carpet continues to smell, but the cold is starting to fade. I don't care about the cold anymore. I'm starting to feel the warmth of my heart beating to the rhythm of the record on the turntable. I will soon be forever, this is an ecstasy of spirit, sadness and joy entwined.

Picking up the glass of water, I gulp the next pill down. I really am on my way now

10 PUBLIC HUMILIATION

I want to die. Now! I want the world to swallow me up. I want it all gone, I want my end now. The shame and the embarrassment is just too much. I'm surrounded by over a hundred people, some close family and some say they are my closest friends, but I feel so alone and detached from them all and I will be detached from them from this moment on. I am on a road of repentance, a crawl of begging and mercy just to be sparingly accepted again. I have never had any self esteem as it is, I really didn't think I could sink any lower than the dark pit I was already in, yet here I am plunging at a thousand miles an hour into a pit of pure waking hell.

The room's spinning and I want to throw up. It's a Thursday evening at the Kingdom Hall, we are half way through the two hour programme and this is the point where it will all happen. Only a few people are aware of what is about to happen and I can't believe I've got here to face this travesty. I've walked two miles to be faced with ritual humiliation and to spend the next few months in public exile.

I feel such a cold chill running down my back. Why did I sit with my mum half way down the hall right in the middle of all these people? I am very aware that the next few minutes are going to be the most degrading of my life this far.

At the front of the hall, someone steps up onto the platform and up to the microphone. There's to be a short announcement from one of the elders. It's a sure sign to everyone that something is about to go down. I've seen this happen many times before, a shock announcement followed by a collective intake of breath by everyone.

One of the elders steps up to the microphone and with absolute assuredness and confidence announces my name followed by the words "has been disassociated". There's a collective sigh and a flurry of whispers that reach out across the church hall. That hustle of low voices and whispers sends waves through my skull and I can feel a million eyes suddenly turn their attention to me. Why won't the earth swallow me up? It takes all of my strength to not just burst out in tears. I pick a focal point on the back of the plastic seat in front of me and stare at it, not daring to move my gaze either way in case I catch a pair of those accusing and disgusted judgemental eyes looking back at me.

After what seems like an eternity of silence from the platform, finally the elder moves away and normal service is resumed. I look to my baby brother who doesn't understand what is happening, he's only ten after all. I refuse to look at my sister. I know even without looking at her that she is loving every moment of this, the ripping divide between my mum and I is much to her enjoyment and satisfaction. I can't look at my mum either. I know she will be devastated at this humiliation, more so because what the congregation thinks of my mum is my mum's chief concern.

Everybody here knows how those few words from the platform by an elder triggers the actions of every person in that room. Every Jehovah's Witness knows that trigger and what it means. I am to be shunned. No-one is allowed to talk to me. I am to come to each church gathering, three times a week for a few months being completely ignored. Even outside the church, my association is to be cut off. No-one is allowed to have anything to do with me until such a time that the elders decide I have shown enough remorse to be graciously allowed back into the church and associated with once again. I must be the last person to arrive at church, so that I don't embarrass someone into accidently talking to me, I must also be the first person to leave for the same reason. Everyone I know in my life, except for the people at work, worship at this Hall. Even my family that I live with will have to minimise if possible, their interaction with me.

It is just a few months since I returned from my week away in South Wales. When I arrived home the only chance of light in my life was the prospect of getting a letter from my beloved Katie. After our week together I couldn't wait to be lifted by what she would say to me, seeing as we had promised ourselves that we would marry. I had no regrets that I hadn't agreed to have sex with her, to have the promise of her love for the rest of my life wasn't even a compromise, it seemed like a beautiful inevitability.

A couple of days since my return from Cardiff I was incredibly anxious to get that first letter. I was in such a dark place and needed lifting from the pit I found myself in. Everyone around me noticed how quiet I was since I got back.

Each morning was tinged with a possible reprieve if that letter with her amazing perfume just dropped through the letterbox, yet each day it didn't. I started to wonder after a few days if my mum had stolen the letter to stop me interacting with Katie, but that didn't make much sense, even though it was highly likely. Katie and I had wrote between two and three letters a week to each other, so it was starting to seem very strange that nearly a week had gone by and there was still no sign of anything coming to me.
By the end of that week I was seriously wondering what could have possibly happened. There was nothing from Katie.

It had been over a week since I had come back from South Wales when my mum asked to speak to me in the dining room with my grandmother in tow. They sat me down and asked me if I had anything to say to them. They had noticed that I had been quiet and down since returning from Cardiff and asked if there was anything I needed to say to them. I had absolutely nothing I wanted to say to them and I told them so.

My mum then produced a letter and straight away I could smell the perfume. My initial reaction was that my mum had stolen a letter from Katie addressed to me. "I knew it" I thought and my mum asked me again if I was sure that I had nothing to say to her. I told my mum that she has stolen my personal possession, a letter addressed to me and that really did mean I had no intention of any dialogue with my mum at all. My mum said the letter was addressed to her, yet she wouldn't let me see it or read it.

The letter prompted my mum going to the elders, which prompted an investigation by the elders which led to me having a full interrogation.

Elder interrogation is the worst bullying I've ever been subjected to. Three elderly male elders, all of them telling me that out of love they will discipline me, but in order to be "fair" they have to know every fact of my experiences from the week I spent with Katie in South Wales. They didn't want to roughly know what I had done, no, instead they wanted a minute by minute, blow by blow full run down of the entire week in every possible and sordid detail. At first I refused as I saw it as none of their business to go to that level of sexual detail, but they insisted that my very life was being judged and I became fearful and caved in to the pressure they applied.

The bizarre reality was, that I had never been baptised, even by seventeen (which is quite old in the religion if you are born into it). That meant that I had not as yet committed myself fully to the church. I felt only about 95 percent sure of what I believed and I thought it dishonest to make a life pledge when I still had that 5 percent of doubt. My sister who is two years younger than I recently got baptised, but I was only concerned as to how a fifteen year old can possibly make that kind of commitment. I knew my sister, I knew the main reason she got baptised was to please not because she had any idea that it was truth or that it was an honest and truthful lifetime commitment. My sister also had not a shred of decency either, which made her promise through baptism even more dubious from my point of view. It was too big a decision for me at seventeen, a decision I could only make if I was forever willing to commit to that promise.

The interrogation by the elders was bizarre because it was as though I was being tried as a baptised witness, even though I wasn't one, as though I was betraying a promise that I had never made.

There was so much sordid detail I had to go through reciting the events of that week in Cardiff that it took three evenings for me just talking to go through the whole week. My intent to slow down time and live every moment of every minute of that entire week was working against me as I could remember every single detail of the entire period. The elders wouldn't let me leave anything out, even when I tried and skipped over what Katie and I did sexually with each other's bodies, they insisted they had the full intricate detail. Everything that was pure, wholesome and beautiful from that week had been painstakingly taken to pieces and analysed and then stamped as absolute filth.

It was only on the second day that I felt any real shame when I saw my friend and chaperone go through the same interrogation at the same time. I wasn't allowed to talk to him. It was the first time I realised that the only wrong here, was putting him in a bad situation that he didn't deserve to be in. That was a bad oversight on my part.

The interrogation finished with the elders asking if I regretted my actions. I didn't regret the most pure, beautiful and amazing thing that had ever happened in my miserable existence. I certainly didn't regret asking Katie to marry me and I was determined that our love would be forever. I just wanted to talk to Katie, hear that she was ok and tell her how much I missed and still loved her. I couldn't help but wonder about the hell she was likely being put through by elders from her congregation. Katie was baptised, she had made that promise, to the church as well as to me. So she would very likely get a harsher punishment than me, although how without resorting to physical violence that could be possible is beyond me.

In the end the elders decided in their wisdom that I didn't show regret so therefore I was not only guilty but unrepentant. The full penalty that could be put upon me therefore was decided on unanimously. I was to be banished. Part of the judgement was brought about because I lied to my mum and the elders. I took that very personally as I don't lie. I never lied to my mother, I didn't see it was any of their business what I had done so had nothing to say. I never denied anything at any time. But as with the whole matter, that didn't seem to make any difference. Refusing to have sex, didn't make any difference, telling the truth for hours on end to a bunch of old perverts didn't make any difference. The greatest lesson learned? The truth in "the truth" gets you nowhere, in the Jehovah's Witnesses society only lies and playing the political game actually get you anything. I was not going to compromise my heart and morals for a set of people that change theirs at a whim.

It has been a couple of weeks of exhausting humiliation and total depression. There is little left in me except for a determination to still be the kindest, warmest person I can regardless of what people do to me.

There is a part of me now asking the question, should I leave this religion. If I was at a 95 percent level of belief before, then my faith has just been knocked down to around 70 percent. The actions of those who say they love me have left me with a huge loss of faith. I feel so loveless. I just want to find my Katie and wrap myself up in her arms again. My mother has outright banned me having any sort of communication with her.

The service carries on. I still want to cry out loud, my knuckles grabbing the plastic chair are white from squeezing. I know there are many still looking at me, I can feel their eyes on me, but as service resumes the attention thankfully starts to turn some in the church hall away to other matters. There's a cold sweat running over me, I still want to throw up. I dare not stand up and rush to the toilet, which would be impossible, I can barely walk anyway and once again more attention would point at me. There's another hour before the end of the service and then I will have to face everyone and leave quickly and in silence.

My thoughts now think about the opportunity to leave this crazy show. I know I have nowhere to go, it's this religion or the streets and I know I wouldn't last a week on the streets. My whole family on my mum's side is so wrapped up in the religion that to them it's black and white, I would have to choose them and the religion or no religion and no family. If I left the religion I would be out the house with nowhere to live and I wouldn't know anyone to fall back on for help. My dad is now a stranger who I see rarely, if at all. He took abuse from us for so long until my sister, my brother and I collectively decided we didn't want to go and see him anymore after of course lots of persuasion from my family and the religion. Now I am in my father's shoes, now I will be shunned and ignored by everyone I know. I suppose there is a certain poetic justice to it. I should think for myself more and not blindly follow the herd. That way of life has brought me here.

I have no choice. I have to work towards my repentance, I have to comply. My inner self, my independence will have to die.

11 NO RETURN

Once again the record finishes and I need to change it. I'm half way through the album and I've taken five pills, I need to speed things up a bit.

The wind howls with a sound of chill around the caravan. The evening is darkening along with my mood. There's a part of me that wonders why I used to carry on, why I didn't get to this point many years ago. That public humiliation was over three years ago and yet I let myself carry on. I protected my inner self and I don't understand why. Why is there still a spark that rebels and wants to prove that a good person can win against the bastards? Why do I fight to still be honest, to be good, to be kind, caring and loving when everyone thinks those qualities are weaknesses? Why do I care?

I don't want to spoil the perfect moment. I'm getting through the neatly set line of white pills and now again the music starts to play on the third side of the album. I pick up pill number six. I'm really in the thick of it now and it is all just beautiful. My face is damp from all the tears pouring, my heart lifts and plunges like a boat on choppy waters. My breathing rises and falls and my eyes wane and dim. I just want to sleep. I love the darkness. The only way to cope with it is to embrace it and the darkness has such beauty and perfection. I can feel it's warm inviting arms, the embrace that will keep me warm and safe. Where I am going, I will fear nothing, I will need nothing, I will be forever wrapped in darkness.

I fill up my water cup and with another drink I swallow the sixth pill.

12 HERE WE GO AGAIN

This is like Déjà vu. I'm in the smaller second room in the Kingdom Hall in front of the same three elders again and this time I'm on a completely different charge. The room is fusty and cold. A little electric heater is all that is trying to break through the icy air in the little used room.

As it was last time, my mum is sat next to me. I can't believe I'm in this situation again. The circumstances are different but the tone and everything else seems the same. I'm a little different, in fact even though I know I should be humble and quiet in front of my peers, I'm actually extremely angry and annoyed.

I served my time. It was a few months I had to spend being shunned, going to the church services without talking to anyone, sitting at the back and showing I wanted back into the fold. I suppose what worked against me was the lack of remorse. I still believed I acted out of love with Katie which I would likely under similar circumstance do the same again. Except I wouldn't be doing anything with Katie, I had lost all contact with her. My mum immediately banned me from having any contact with her at all after my disassociation. No letters, no messages, nothing. I tried to get one of the girls in the congregation to write to her before my banishment, but my mum got wind of it and stopped it straight away.

I started to question my constant honesty. Anyone else would just disobey any rules, lie their way through it and do as they please, but I couldn't do anything, because if I was asked, I would always tell the truth. I was my own worst enemy. After a few months my desire to talk to Katie under the strain of absolute heartache, deep depression and loneliness got the better of me. I managed to stay one evening at my uncle's house on my own. None of my mum's houses ever had a telephone, I had never been in an environment of having one, but my Uncle did. So after two hours of arguing with myself that one night, I plucked up the courage to ring Katie's house in Cardiff. Her dad initially answered the phone and just passed me straight through to her. The next ten minutes were pure hell. Instead of finding out that because she was baptised that she had been through the same hell as me, she had actually met another young Jehovah's witness man and was in a serious relationship with him. How could she have met someone if she wasn't allow to talk to anyone, how did she fall in love with someone so quickly? I was so shocked I couldn't talk on the telephone hardly at all. She hardly remembered who I was, after just three months of being apart. The woman who joined me in a promise to marry, struggled to remember who I was.

I felt so guilty afterwards for stealing my Uncle's telephone line under a veil of deceit. I confessed to my Uncle and offered to pay the phone bill and I was willing to accept any punishment due. Thankfully, he just told me not to do it again and never said anything more of it.

I eventually served my time like a good Christian and got re-instated back into the congregation after a few long months. Nothing was ever the same though. I was tarnished. Nearly everyone treated me like I was damaged goods. Families were weary of me, youngsters were told either to stay away from me or limit their time with me. It was also harder to get the little jobs I had before in the congregation. Serving my time was not a clean slate like it was supposed to be. Every privilege had to be earned even harder than before.

That was over a year ago.

A couple of months ago a new family moved into the area and into the congregation. The family had a 14 year old daughter that the young lads of my age really found attractive. The pickings of potential female partners in our congregation has always been slim, so a new girl was always going to attract attention. I liked her a little, except for the fact that she was just too young for me and of course I wasn't allowed in any way shape or form to have anything to do with the opposite sex. A couple of my friends though would take any opportunity to pal around with her. She was a bit of a tomboy, so would happily kick a football around or try a bit of rock climbing with us. She actually became one of the lads and probably because her family were new to the congregation, the whole family treated me fairly and not as damaged like many others in the congregation did.

Then just over a week ago, I got the tragic news that she had been knocked over by a car and was in hospital. The news knocked me sideways. I waited a couple of days until getting the all clear to go to the hospital and visit and as soon as that moment came I went to see her.

That first time I visited she didn't look as bad as I feared. She was in a private room outside the main ward. The whole place was a constant buzz of people constantly coming and going, chatting, hugging and showing support for their family. I had cycled after work in the cold and dark, five miles to get to the hospital. When I sat down next to her, her whole face lit up and she grabbed hold of my hand and held it tight.

For over three hours that evening I sat there holding her hand. I felt really awkward. I had a history that many in the congregation would have the attitude that it made me trouble and not to be trusted with anyone of the opposite sex. I knew that many in the congregation had that frame of mind and when some of them walked into that hospital room and saw me sat next to her holding her hand, I could feel the disapproval. Those looks really made me sweat. Several times that evening her mum came up to me and told me how grateful they were that I was there holding her hand and that it had really picked her up by me just being there. I felt I couldn't move away. Between the firm hold of my hand and her mother's desire to see me stay there, I thought I was performing a greater good that surpassed my selfish embarrassment.

By around 9:30pm, most of the visitors had been and gone and there were just the mum and dad and I left in the hospital room. A doctor came in to update them on recent tests and diagnosis and for no more than two minutes, they stepped outside the room with the door open and talked about how they were to progress with treatment. I could hear nearly every word just outside the door.

It was getting time to leave. When the parents came back in, I said my goodbyes and pulled away my hand from that still tight grip.

The cycle home was cold, wet and full of sorrow. At the same time I felt really proud of myself that despite how uncomfortable I felt, I knew I was doing good just by being there and being supportive. The girl's mum couldn't thank me enough.

I wanted to get back to the hospital again as soon as I could, but didn't want to intrude, so I kept leaving messages to ask when it would be convenient for me to visit again. It was a few days until I was able to because of church commitments. Church takes up so much of one's time, it can be frustrating.

Eventually I was able to visit again and cycled up to the hospital on my own as before. She had been moved out of that single room and was in the general ward with five other beds. Once again I was told by her mum how she picked up once I got there. Typically there were less people visiting and in the 3 hours I was there only a couple of groups turned up for a half hour at a time. She was obviously still doped up a little I thought as she still wasn't totally with it. But enough that we could still chat and have a joke or two. Again as before, her mum was full of thanks for me being there and supporting them for most of the evening. Her mum even asked if I would watch over her while they went and found something to eat somewhere as they hadn't had any food for hours.

That evening I went home so pleased that I had not only been of great help but that they trusted me the way they did and didn't have the same attitude about me as many did in the congregation.

It was only two days later that I was summoned here with my mum, freezing my nuts off and going through the same direct judgement from three elders acting as my judges and executioners. It was massively different this time though as I didn't have a clue what I had been summoned for. Before getting here, I did have a small clue thrown my way. I wanted to arrange another visit to the hospital, but my mum told me that I had been told to stay away, not asked, not even a "thanks for your support but…". The threat was clear, I was told to stay away. Then when I arrived with my mum, the girl's father was already at the Kingdom Hall and he was extremely angry. He had always been such a placid and gentle man, but when he saw me he looked like he wanted to kill me. One of the elders actually had to constrain him and partially hold him back when I arrived.
That welcome from someone who only a couple of days ago was hugging me makes me so nervous. What the hell is going on?

One of the elders starts by asking me what I think and feel about the girl. Then another asks more probing questions about whether I had any attraction to her, if I found her sexually arousing. I should feel uncomfortable, but I've been here before. Three married men that think that anything to do with love is also only about sex and that every young man is a potential sexual predator. I tried to answer honestly while simultaneously trying to figure out what was happening.

Through my head are flashing images of the girl's father, angry and mad at me when I arrived. I'm tempted to think that someone has told him an exaggerated story of Katie and I and he has become paternally defensive and accusing me of saying something inappropriate to his daughter.

Having my mum beside me just makes me more nervous. No matter what I am to be accused of, I know my mum will never side with me. She never does. I have spent my life being guilty before being proven innocent. I see other parents that protect their awful children knowing full well what little gits they are, I got that parent in reverse.

After two hours of intense interrogation, answering barrages of questions and being scrutinised over every movement I've made over the last two weeks, the reason behind all this cloak and dagger questioning finally comes out.

I'm being accused of raping the girl in her hospital bed. Not once but twice.
I'm accused that in that space of two minutes when she was in the private room, when her mum and dad where talking to the doctor outside, with the door open, I climbed into her hospital bed and forced myself into her. Then a few days later on the open hospital ward, with five other full beds in the room and nurses walking about, when her mum went for something to eat, I did it again.

Once again in my life I want the world to swallow me up. Once again I want to just stop being and just die on the spot. I think of myself as a hopeless romantic. All I want in my life is to be loved and be wrapped up in a cloak of love and affection and return in equal measure that love, warmth, empathy and sensuality. This just typifies how totally alone I am, in the fact that the people around me that should know me deeply, have no idea who I am. Rape is the most despicable act that I could ever imagine and is the polar opposite of the love and spirituality I want to feel when with someone.

I try and ask the elders, how physically I'm supposed to have been able to perform such acts without casting any suspicion or doubt. Even the physical aspect of undressing, doing the deed in complete silence and returning to a default pose once again with no sign of struggle, mess or loss of composure in such a short time span seems a feat of impossibility. But that seems irrelevant, as the girl not only said it happened, but named me by name as the person that did it.

I'm devastated. I can feel my brain firing at a million flashes a second. I'm struck between the preposterous accusation and the realisation of why her dad is so angry with me. Those parents would never doubt their daughter and they never should. I can feel their pain and sheer anger. At the same time I have a feeling that no matter the evidence, I am going to be damned and for the most despicable of crimes.

The elders start to wrap it up. I want to cry out and shout with total anguish as loud as I can and fall to the floor in a flood of tears, but I fight it. Everyone stands up. I can hardly raise myself off the chair. I'm spent, emotionally drained to the core with no desire to even breathe anymore. I feel that no matter what I do or say, to these people I am a filthy and disgusting pervert and guilty without need for fairness or honesty, I am the witch that needs to burn.

As everyone makes towards the door, I cannot feel my feet. All I can think of is whether or not her father is still behind that door, knowing what he wants to do to me. The door opens and my mum walks through into the main hall. The evening is late and the temperature has dropped further. The elders say they are going to stay and carry on to discuss between them what I have told them and my mum and I are asked to leave and go home. I stick my head around the door into the main room to thankfully see that no one else is here.

My mum and I walk across the hall as the door behind us closes. I can't hang on any longer and my knees nearly buckle and the tears just start flowing uncontrollably. Unusually, my mum puts her arm around me and tries to comfort me as we walk out the Kingdom Hall into the car park. My mum looks at me with my red swollen eyes and distorted mumblings and says, "I think I'm starting to understand you after tonight. You really did love Katie didn't you? Well, I believe you're telling the truth and I will stick by you".

13 NO RETURN

I remember that cold night. It was colder than tonight and the Kingdom Hall didn't feel any warmer a spiritual place than this caravan does now. There's a sudden shock like an electric connection between then and now sparking directly into my swollen, heavy dark heart.

That poor girl. If I wasn't the guilty party, then who was it? The elders never went to the police which they should have done. I remember wishing they had so that at least I could have been cleared with professionally collected evidence. As with many matters concerning Jehovah's witnesses, everything stays internal and secret. I never talked to her again even though I saw her twice a week at church. It was quite clear that she was never the same again mentally, whether through the accident or through anything that may have happened in her hospital bed.

I start to wonder how I got through that torment for a second time. It seems that for some stupid stubborn reason, I just keep getting back up again, returning back to the ring for another round. Why did I do that, was it habit, stubbornness, or just a lack of nerve? Probably just fear of the unknown.

I have wanted to be where I am now so many times. I've wanted on so many occasions to just let it all go, to just let it stop and go to sleep. Finally I am doing it, finally I'm well on the final road to proper peace and the bliss of ignorant nothingness.

I pick up another pill. This is number seven. I know now that I'm well into my journey and can no longer return. That will to survive, that ability to bounce back is fast becoming irrelevant. I'll soon be at double dosage. There is no return.

I pick up the water. Pop another white pill on my tongue and take another drink. The love I wish to find in death will soon be with me.

14 THE CURE

Highs and lows. That is the rollercoaster that is my life. A few hours ago I could cry with a sense of joy, fulfilment, love, heartbreak and loneliness. Now I stand on junction 29 of the M1 at two in the morning trying to decide where to go next.

The summer cool night air fills my lungs. It feels fresh and clean despite being on a main road. I throw my rucksack on the grass verge and take a few minutes to decide what I'm going to do. This motorway junction is huge. It's about a mile all the way around the roundabout. The M1 runs north / south underneath it and junctions come off for Clay Cross, Chesterfield, Bolsover, or Mansfield. Many choices, many destinations laid out before me and yet I feel like I only have two. Run away or go home and face the music.

Today has been a massive sacrifice and a stand for what I believe is right for me and there are going to be great consequences for those decisions.
A few months ago, I had the opportunity to go to my first gig. It was in Sheffield at the Leadmill to see The

Wonderstuff do a gig promoting their debut album The Eight Legged Groove Machine. I loved the album, I thought it was so witty and clever. A friend of mine who once was a Jehovah's Witness that had stopped going to church a couple of years ago, was the one that got me the ticket and was going to drive me up to Sheffield.

I'm nineteen years old, still living at home and I have to ask my mum if it's ok to go. The biggest problem is that I have a strict eleven pm curfew that I've broken twice already. The first time was after a bible study and my mentor had to spend an hour convincing my mum that at five passed eleven, it was his fault I hadn't got back in time and I should be let into the house to sleep. The second time, I was one minute late and had to sleep on a bench in the village square all night in a t-shirt and shorts.

To be able to get back into the house and into bed, I therefore needed permission to go out later than eleven. Actually, I needed permission for everything I wanted to do anyway, the "while you live under this roof..." set of dictates my mum always put me under.

Needless to say, mostly because of the company I was going to be with, an ex Jehovah's Witness, my mum refused and told me under no circumstances was I allowed to go.

It was a few weeks later that I noticed in the local record shop that my favourite band where doing a special one day festival south of London. It was an all-day event with Lush, James, All About Eve supporting, then the Cure playing the headliner slot. I have loved the Cure for years and have been totally wrapped up their new album called

Disintegration over the past year, an album that perfectly reflected my sense of overall loss, loneliness and isolation so well. I had sensibly weighed up the situation. The tickets that were offered in the record shop not only included the ticket for the event at the Crystal Palace Bowl, but a coach trip there and back as well. I could travel on my own, so no bad company to be influenced by, be safely escorted there and back with a reliable coach company and safely attend my first ever gig in as much safety and isolation as was possible. My mum couldn't object surely and if she did, this time I would put my foot down and go anyway.

I bought the ticket from the record shop and kept it secret from my mum. The plan was to tell her a couple of days before so if she objected there was little she could do about it. Typically when it did come to the day of telling her, my mum told me I couldn't go. When I told her how careful I had been in covering every scenario in order to be safe and not have any bad influences with me, she didn't care and told me that "I was going and listening to the devils music and to also worship idols". My mum didn't have a clue about music at all, what she did with those ABBA records years before was a typical example. Everything had a demonic influence according to my mum except for classical music, despite the obvious debauchery of all those famous composers she pretended to like. A logic I just never understood.

My mum told me I was not allowed to go. So I told her I was going anyway, despite her protestations. My mother's reaction was to give me notice, I had a month to get out the house for good.

At first I didn't believe what she had threatened, threats

like that happened often, I was a constant disappointment. But this time I realised something was different. This time she really meant it and I got a strong sense that I would not be able to reason with her, there was never any reasoning with my mum.

That totally killed any excitement about the gig before I even got to the day.
The temperature is just right even though it's past two in the morning. I could just curl up in the hedgerow and sleep for a couple of hours. I know if I decide to just go and run away from here that I would be best starting now, get as much distance from the local area as possible. I know too many people around here, the congregation is too large and it would be too easy to be spotted and maybe even taken home against my will.

Stupidly I've had my best opportunities in the past three hours to slip away. I've just come from the south of London, I would have been best trying from there to find a place to squat. But that is exactly it, I know my weaknesses and a man of the world I most certainly am not. I can hardly feed myself, I never cook, I have no real concept of money or any desire for it. In London I would be eaten alive. I would likely be dead and another statistic in less than a week. Or is that just the fear arguing with me?

I kick at the tall grass at the side of the road, frustrated with myself, with my lack of adventure and daring. Disobeying my mum's orders and going to the gig was an extreme of daring for me and one that has already got to get me into all sorts of problems. I feel stuck, like thick treacle is grabbing hold of my feet and stopping me from walking. I don't want to go home, to the hell I have to face every day, to a faith I have no confidence in, to family and friends that I know will turn their back on me if I left the religion. At the same time I don't have the courage to go anywhere else. This world outside of the religion is so alien to me. I have been cocooned all my life from the outside world to the point that I know nobody in it and know nothing of it, except for the people at work and I have nothing in common with them. Leaving home or running away leaves me not just without a roof over my head, but leaves me with nobody at all.

Once again I'm doing that yo yo thing. Up and down, high and low. This morning I got out of the house before seven am. I made sure that my mum would not see what I was wearing, although I'm not dressed that outlandish really. Last year I had bought a suit from Burton's. It was light grey and very unusual. It had zip pockets and the jacket only hung down to just above my hips. It certainly wasn't traditional and I loved it. My mum of course hated it because it wasn't normal and tried first to tell me I couldn't wear it to church, even though it was very smart, and then tried to get the Elders to tell me I wasn't allowed to wear it. A couple of Elders did have a quiet word with me a couple of times, telling me that I was drawing attention to myself by wearing that suit, but I ignored them. Most of the Elders to me had become either politicians fighting over each other for power, or dirty perverts dragging people through hell for their own kicks. I had no respect at all for most of them. Needless to say, I took no notice. How can a piece of cloth make god more or less loving or acceptable. I knew my heart, so everything external was irrelevant.

Before going out the house this morning, I had tried to use sticky gel to "punk" up my hair and mess it up a bit. It worked quite well, especially for a first time amateur. Thankfully I got out of the house without being seen by my mum. I caught the bus from the village, five miles into town and waited at the pick-up point for the coach. While standing there, two young girls of around seventeen arrived and just went wild when they saw me as they thought I was the spitting image of Robert Smith, the singer from the Cure. It was seven thirty in the morning and they were already partially drunk. I didn't know what to do with myself, so I tried to play along as shyly and quietly as I could.

I watched quite horrified at the two of them get more and more drunk through the morning. One of them was pregnant and I thought she shouldn't have been getting drunk in her obvious state of development. By the time we were half way to London, she was throwing up in a plastic bag and throwing the full bag out the window of the coach. While a part of me was intrigued by the two very independent, loud and confident girls, they also frightened me greatly at their destructive personalities. Part of me liked the small amount of attention they gave me and another part of me wanted to put some distance away from them.

I tried to just go with the flow instead and just let the day take its natural course. When we got to the Crystal Palace Bowl and got off the coach, the two girls where insistent that I stayed with them all day. They dragged me by the hand up to the entrance and the security checks. Being the typical sensible old head on young shoulders that I was and also because I was from Derbyshire, home of the tight arse and money miser, I had taken a large rucksack full of orange juice, sandwiches, crisps and all the things a hungry boy in the wild would need. Of course as soon as I got dragged to the entranceway a security man asked to go through my bag with an intense inspection. I stood there thinking I was going to get my bag taken off me for taking in food and drink, as the two girls ran off in a flurry of excitement and left without me.

The natural order of things had made its decision, I was on my own for the rest of the day.

I got into the venue with all my belongings intact. In the Crystal Palace Bowl was a world of wonder. Thousands of young and excited people, some with the most amazing styles, backcombed hair, punk or black gothy clothes. It was an amazing sight. I was in awe at the beauty of some of those people, girls and boys. They looked so other worldly and creatively individual. I was so jealous of their freedom. I wanted to have that creative freedom myself, I wanted to express myself in my own unique way.

The day was a beautiful one. The sun shone through a totally clear blue sky. Occasionally a huge aeroplane on its way to one of the London airports would fly low overhead. The trees in the park where full, green, lush and still as there was little to no breeze to move them. Many people had brought picnic baskets and blankets with them and spread themselves over the grass. Everywhere I looked the views were both a fantastic experience and a reminder of how utterly lonely I was.

Once again I made sure to appreciate every moment, to capture every second of the day and to not miss a thing or not take note of every detail that surrounded me.

Many smells drifted over the air. There were stalls selling beer and lager, with looked more frothy head than liquid and the prices were stupidly expensive. I was glad I had my made up bottles of squash. Other stalls sold burgers and chips, which filled the air with hot greasy temptation. Again I was quite happy with my collection of sandwiches, cheese and pickle of course.

As the first band came on and the music started to blare out from the huge array of speakers on scaffolding either side of the park, huge bellows of smoke was released from the stage down at the bottom of the hill. As the smoke drifted up the hill I could smell the sweetness from it. As I looked around there were a lot of people smoking which filled the air with wisps of cigarette smoke, but there was another smell I didn't recognised. It was a very pleasant smell I had not smelled before. As I looked around I noticed it came from people smoking, but it wasn't cigarettes. I was totally shocked as I worked out what it likely was. It was cannabis.

I was so shocked that people could be so without shame as they made no attempt to hide it, we were in the open air on a bright sunny summer afternoon. I couldn't believe that drugs were so open and so easy. I had images of drugs being sold and used in dark sleazy alleyways by bums and tramps. That was the world I was warned about.

Then the music picked me up out of my ignorant stare, a beautiful voice that floated about above loud smashing and thrashing guitars and drums. It was the first band playing called Lush and I was sure I had heard one of their songs before on the John Peel radio show late one night. It fitted the atmosphere and the situation perfectly. It stopped my walkabout for a half hour while I stood transfixed to the music blasting out across the summer air. What a perfect moment.

Once Lush finished playing I continued my long walk around the whole park. Part of me wanted to bump into the two girls from the coach again, but I knew with thousands of people being there that I was unlikely to do so. As lonely as I felt I was determined to experience everything with a full array of my senses and to not miss a moment despite the crippling loneliness I felt, ironically surrounded by so many fellow music lovers.

James were the next band on and for some reason they didn't really do anything for me. They played ok, but the music for some reason just didn't make much of an impact with me. So I carried on my tour of the park.
When All About Eve came on to play, I had finished my tour and had picked a really cool spot to sit down and enjoy my sandwiches and crisps. I knew a few songs by All About Eve and I thought I might enjoy their music, but again, the music left me unmoved.

When All about Eve finished playing, it seemed to take forever for the stage to be cleared and then set up again for The Cure. I was really looking forward to seeing them play. I had followed their music for a few years and just loved the whole image that went with their music. The sun was just starting to disappear from the park as the Cure came on stage and started to play. Everything was just perfect, except for being on my own. I always wondered why I have always felt that an experience not shared is an experience halved.

The Cure played for three and a half hours as the late afternoon turned into the evening and the park got darker and darker until we were all in the pitch dark experiencing something magical. Because the gig was to promote the album Disintegration, they played the whole album, an album I knew backwards and just adored. It took everything I had through the evening to not to just cry through every song.

For nearly the whole day I had managed through some minor miracle to forget the horror that was waiting for me once I got home and the consequences I would soon face. It was only when the Cure finished their encores and all the parks floodlights came on that reality hit me like a punch to the face. One of the best days of my life was not only coming to an end, I was returning to a home to people that didn't want me there anymore in a congregation that didn't want me anymore.

It was at that moment that my first thoughts of escape on my terms entered my head. I was more than a hundred and fifty miles from home. No-one really knew where I was. For all my mums concerns she never asked for details of where I was going, or what time I was to be home. All those previous disagreements were about control, not love or concern. If I had disappeared right then and there, just slipped off into the London suburbs, no-one would care.

But I'm a coward and have always been a coward. I know there are homeless people that would give everything they have to live one more day in a warm, dry house with food in the cupboards. I feared the outside world that the religion warned me of that I knew nothing about. If I believed everything I was told, everyone who is not a

Jehovah's Witness is a thief, a liar, an immoral, debauched and selfish animal ready to devour anyone that is innocent. I feared I wouldn't last a day in such a world.

The long trip back on the quiet coach was two hours of internal battling with myself, fighting for an answer or the courage to just run. The two girls that I befriended on the way down to the concert were both fast asleep on the coach all the way back.

When we got near to junction 29 on the motorway, I asked if I could get dropped off on the roundabout. From here it is just three miles home, whereas it would be a 5 mile walk home from the centre of Chesterfield where I was picked up from all those hours ago. It hadn't occurred to anyone else to ask to be dropped off somewhere until I asked, which started off a mass negotiation between passengers and driver. Because of those frantic negotiations when I got dropped off, no-one really noticed.

Now I have got to the point where I don't know what the easiest or smartest thing to do is. Running away and not facing my mother seems to be growing as the easier thing to do. Running away gives me control back. I know the braver thing to do is meet my accuser head on and face the consequences like a grown up. The sensible thing to do is go home. From there I can plan where to go, make arrangements and take measured steps rather than rash impulsive ones.

Sometimes I hate my sensible logic. Regardless of the pain, I'm going home.

15 OUROBORUS

I'm so confused. Why am I here again? This does not make any sense to me, how did I end up in this same situation? I look around at the faces, all familiar and yet different. That smell of cheap aftershave, over used perfume and old people's talc. Everywhere is quiet and formal as the speaker talks from the platform right down the front of the hall. Every so often the odd face turns around and catches a glimpse of me. I'm so ashamed and yet so glad to see these familiar faces once again.

This warm familiarity fills me with a feeling of love, yet I'm so conflicted because I know it's a shallow love. When that glimpse catches my eye, I feel familiar and yet once again ashamed. It reminds me of the consequences of being banished from the church years ago and having to sit at the back where no-one was allowed to talk to me. I sat then in shame and I sit now humbled and ashamed.

I also feel internally ashamed of being a coward, like I have taken the easy way out. I have betrayed myself. All these people that turned their backs on me, that never cared where I was or how I was or if I was alive will gloat inwardly that they have brought me back into the fold with their "tough love".

I can only remember snippets of the past two hours. Two hours of feeling like the walking dead and walking in an almost drunken daze.

The talk is over from the platform and everyone stands to their feet picking up the church song book and opening it to the designated hymn. Two or three introductory notes ring out over the loudspeaker to start everyone singing. Within seconds of standing up, I recognise the tune. I haven't heard a church song in months. The music rips my heart straight into two and I just burst into uncontrollable tears, so much that I can't stand anymore and fall to my seat.

I have missed this and every person here, even though I know I'm a traitor to myself.

16 A NEW CHAPTER

It was seven months ago when my mum finally threw me out. I nervously searched out my dad at the local pub in the next village and he gave me a room in his already very crowded home in which to live. I couldn't believe how kind that was to do such a thing. The whole of his family suffered as his three girls and one very young boy had to all then share one bedroom together in order to squeeze me in. It was very crowded. Even more amazing was how accepting my step mum was. She really didn't have to do anything, in fact she most likely didn't want me around, a reminder of all the horrible things my mum had done not only to my dad, but to his whole family.

Within a couple of weeks of living there, I was starting to question my old life in the church. My family and friends at the church already started to look at me like damaged goods, even more than they already done before. My dad was disfellowshipped from the Jehovah's Witnesses. He had been baptised as a youngster and taken that oath. When my mum wanted shut of him, she made my dad's life so much hell that he left. Later my mum wanted a divorce to get maintenance money from my dad. In the church, only adultery is recognised as reason to annul a marriage, so she accused him of adultery. Initially, my dad didn't even know anyone to commit adultery with, but as the proceedings went along, he met my step mum and capitulated. The church then disfellowshipped my dad from his capitulation at court of admittance to adultery.

Many years ago he went through the same shame as I did. Everyone he knew turned their back on him and shunned him, except for his own family. His parents and brothers didn't shun him as they were supposed to. My dad never made any attempt to stay in the church though, so he didn't go through that extra humiliation that I did.

Because I was living with my dad, I was marked in the congregation on top of all my other misdemeanours. Because my mum had thrown me out, regardless of what people thought of my mum, nobody wanted to get involved and so kept their distance. At that time I was still going to church at least twice a week, but the response I got there was cold. At each church meeting I sat on my own away from my mum, I was walking nearly four miles to church and four miles back again to my dad's house. Going to church was also digging at my conscience. My dad had gone through hell from the hands of the very church that I was visiting. Even some 13 years on, he was still ignored in the streets by people he once knew and was close to and once called friends. My dad had so kindly taken me into his home where his family struggled to live and I was repaying him by rubbing his face in a religion that public humiliated him. I decided it was time I grew up fast and found out if the outside world really was as mean and evil as my previous 20 years had taught me.

NINE PILLS

I stopped going to church.

I was 20 years old and still a virgin. Apart from Katie 3 years before, I had never even kissed a girl. I was naïve in the ways of love, I just knew that I would love and adore someone completely if I was lucky enough to get the chance. That chance wasn't very long in the waiting. My eldest step sister who was at college had a friend who she thought she could match me up with. I was in a totally new world that I just didn't understand at all. My mum's house had always been religious to the extreme. If a swear word was heard on the television, it was instantly switched off. If a breast was shown or even a hint of a sex act even fully clothed was on the television, it was switched off. Sex was never mentioned except to highlight the filth of the world outside.

My dad's house was completely different. My stepmum would walk around her house in just a t-shirt and no bra and she was not at all small chested. I was always having to look at the floor all the time as I just wanted to stare at her breasts wobbling around all the time. My step mum and dad would jokingly just say they were going for a walk and go into the local countryside trail to have sex together in peace and everyone in the house knew what they were doing. The two older step girls both talked about how much sex they were having all the time. It was an environment that totally shocked me and thrilled me at the same time. I didn't know if the rest of the world was like that or not, the church certainly warned me it was.

My oldest step sister and her friend were both sixteen. I was quickly taken to college to meet my step sister's friend and much to my surprise, she liked me and wanted to meet me again. Her name was Amy, she was very pretty and I thought way out of my league. My biggest astonishment was the reaction from my Dad and Stepmum. They just made a big fuss over meeting my first real girlfriend and they teased me with all sorts of sexual innuendo and fun, the type of which I had never heard before, never mind being in the middle of.

I still had a month's worth of wages from my last job and my new parents wouldn't take any board from me, so I felt so financially rich and took Amy out a couple of times for a meal and a drink. Of course I was the perfect gentleman, simply because I didn't expect anything from Amy at all. Any sign of affection or attention was a huge bonus for me, a real honour and privilege to have any attention from Amy at all.

After a couple of weeks of being together, we spent an afternoon in a local park with my Step sister and her boyfriend. It was a beautiful early autumn afternoon. The trees were just beginning to turn, the sun was still quite warm and the air had the slightest chill. My Stepsister was really going to town on the poor boy that lay on the grass beneath her, very heavily kissing and rubbing each other all over through their clothes without a care that Amy and I were lying next to them. Amy was also sat on top of me caught up the mood of the warm afternoon.

I had only stopped going to church a few weeks before and although the situation I found myself in was extremely arousing, I couldn't stop the awareness of where I was. I was only a few hundred yards away from the village, where many members of the congregation lived. I knew it would take just one of those to see me in that situation and my family would be shamed for my actions. While I was aware of that irony, that I seemed to care for a family that didn't seem to show the same affection for me, there was a part of me that didn't want to give them any satisfaction of being able to say to everyone, "I told you he was like that, shameful and selfish, bringing reproach on his family". Needless to say these thought processes worked against the passion of the moment. It still didn't stop Amy rubbing her groin into mine.

I still feared god as well to a certain extent. I had felt damned by god for a long time and although I fought that fear, I mostly felt that I was going to reap the worse judgement from god when the time came.

My step sister and her boyfriend both jumped up to their feet, giggling like a pair of children and told us they were going into the trees to have sex. I was shocked and surprised, was it really that easy? Then my step sister dragged her boyfriend off in the direction of the trees and disappeared.
Amy had a wicked glint in her eye as she continued to kiss me and writhe her hips into mine. She asked me if I wanted to have sex with her.

I didn't know what to do with myself. I was shocked, surprised and excited at the same time. But the situation wasn't romantic at all, in fact it was nothing like what I expected my first time to be. I expected my first time to be with a woman I loved and adored and that loved me wholeheartedly. I had no problem realising that Amy liked me a lot, but I was unsure if she had any feelings for me after only a couple of weeks of being together. It was hardly the romantic wedding night scenario I had dreamed about all my adult life.

Amy could tell I was aroused and into what she was doing. There was a really awkward period of silence. How could I explain in a way she would understand everything that was going off in my head, the excitement, the fear, the disappointment and yet the thrill.

I tried to explain to Amy while she looked at me with that wonderfully wicked smile on her face how I was still actually a virgin and hadn't envisaged losing my cherry on a grassy embankment in the middle of the day. So I asked her if we could wait a couple of weeks so I could set a romantic night up that would be more emotionally fulfilling for the both of us. Thankfully instead of thinking I was a complete idiot, Amy thought I was totally sweet and agreed to wait until I was ready.

I must have told my step sister some time later as it didn't take long for my dad and stepmum to get wind of my romantic proposal and the fact that I turned down popping my cherry, which they found hilarious. It was such a culture shock going from one scenario where I would be practically stoned to death for even looking sexually at a woman to being almost mocked by my new parents for not having sex with a girl. It was so very difficult to stop my head spinning. The most difficult thing I was always aware of, was making sure that by some mistake and miss interpretation, I didn't end up saying or doing something totally inappropriate. That thought frightened the hell out of me.

When my dad and stepmum got word that I planned to have a more romantic setting for losing my virginity, both of them said I could let Amy stay the night with me in my room in their house, my new home. Once again I was blown over by that offer. So many things seemed so wrong with that scenario. Amy was only sixteen, which didn't seem to bother them, they were letting me have sex under their roof, which I couldn't believe that grown-ups could be that liberal and on also that they were goading me to do it as well like a bunch of lads at the pub would. The new world I found myself in was so very, very strange.

I set a date in October. The band Tangerine Dream, who never played in the UK at all since the early seventies, where actually playing in Sheffield, so I bought Amy and I tickets. The idea was to take her out to Sheffield for dinner, go to the concert then go home for a romantic night in. Amy didn't have a clue who Tangerine Dream were, which was fine, I thought the experience would be cultured and interesting. I had loved Tangerine Dream's music for years.

That day was strange, like I had the sword of Damocles hanging over me the whole day. If I went through with my plan, I would be a dead man walking before the next day. I tried not to, but I was carrying that around with me all day. Nobody was pressuring me to lose my virginity other than myself. If I was to become part of the world outside the church, it was pointless dipping my toe in and then saying I don't like it. Many would say, you have to jump in and commit. I certainly was jumping in.

We took the train to Sheffield. Had a dinner for two at Pizza hut, then went to the concert at the City Hall. Sheffield City Hall was big enough for a couple of thousand people, but it was a stretch if a hundred people were actually there for the gig on the night. The venue was practically empty. That suited me, it made the experience more personal. It was great to see Tangerine Dream, although by 1990 they had seriously lost their mojo musically.

Amy really enjoyed the gig, which I was surprised at really. Then to add to the whole strangeness of the day, we missed the last train back to Chesterfield, the concert hadn't even finish that late either. The evening was cold and wet and I thought that I had been extremely lucky to have kept Amy's interest through the evening as it was, missing the last train was going to ruin my lucky streak. So in a moment of madness I got into a black cab and got it to take the two of us the 15 miles home. It cost me a small fortune, but it was warm, dark and kind of adventurous taking a taxi all that way home.

When the cab arrived outside my dad's house I was nervous. I still wasn't sure if my dad was fully allowing Amy to spend the night in my bedroom, it still seemed a very strange and unusual to allow such a thing to happen. But everyone was so relaxed with such adult matters to a point I had no idea what was normal at all anymore.

Amy and I ran out the taxi, through the rain and into the house. The whole family were still awake and in the living room watching television. It almost felt like they were all waiting for us to come home to cheer us on our way. As soon as we got inside and took off our coats we were both faced with giggles and expecting eyes. It was such a ludicrous and strange set of circumstances. I felt so uncomfortable and embarrassed for Amy. I wanted to act really casual about the whole scenario, but I was so very nervous and the roomful of staring, expectant eyes just made my nervousness worse. So I ushered Amy quickly through the room, still half expecting to be stopped when my dad realised that I was going to go through with it and he had changed his mind, or at least my step mum may have. With a red face and a grin I made excuses and into the stairway, dragging Amy by the hand behind me to whoops of cheer and encouragement. Finally Amy and I ended up in the privacy of my small bedroom and the single bed therein and the quiet solitude it provided. Finally we were alone.

I lit a couple of candles and put on some quiet music and nervously tried to take it all slowly and maturely. Yet as much as I tried, the whole scenario was cold, unromantic and was over in a half hour.

I was so disappointed. It just wasn't the loving, caring, empathic and beautiful experience I had always hoped it would be. Sex was actually a bit painful, a bit fumbly, actually quite funny and just didn't have any spiritual awakening at all. I tried to hide the disappointment from Amy as much as I could. It wasn't her first time at all and it seemed to be just another shag to her, so very normal.

My initial disappointment was replaced with a deep, deep sense of death and doom. I had sold my soul for that small moment, I was now damned with god for an eternity. The repercussions with everyone in my life would be profound for such a small and ludicrously pointless half an hour of my life. I really did have a wash of darkness suddenly drown me in that all encompassing reality. I was now spiritually dead.

It was only a week later when Amy and I were going to

spend another night at my dad's home that all hell broke loose. A very late penny dropped in my step mum's head that Amy was only sixteen the same age as her daughter, my step sister. Why that wasn't so blatantly obvious in the first place completely confused and infuriated me. My step sister and Amy where friends because they were at same college and doing the same course together, so that alone would make them the same age in my reckoning. My step mum was furious with me saying that I had deceived the whole family. It would seem that my paranoia about doing something wrong in that strange and alien world was well founded. In the church, although sex was not allowed, many couples got together when the girl was sixteen, many where married by seventeen and eighteen. Amy's age didn't seem a problem to me, I was only nineteen myself.

From that day on, Amy wasn't even allowed at my dad's house anymore, she was barred. Every day I had to get the two buses into Chesterfield and then out to Amy's house, and then back again every evening just to be able to see her. I didn't mind, I got quite close to her and found her to be wonderful company. Just being with her was more than enough for me. I tried to introduce her to my unusual tastes in music and film and for a while everything looked good.

That was until today.

By now I had run out of money, had started a new job in a clothes factory that started early and finished late. I struggled to afford the money and the time to see Amy every evening, although every effort to see her for me was always worth it. Amy always wanted to go out every evening, which usually meant hanging around street corners in the cold and dark with Amy's mates. I just wanted to spend time with her in the warmth of her parent's house after a horrible day at work.

When I knocked on her front door this afternoon, she answered the door looking half excited and half sheepish. Amy wanted to tell me what she was so excited about but was worried about my reaction. She then told me with a glint in her eye and full of childish excitement how her former boyfriend had changed his mind and wanted her back and last night they got back together again. Amy then told me about how much she had always loved him and had missed him the whole of the five months we had been together.

Every word she excitedly spouted was another nail in my flesh. I could feel blood pouring out of me. What had I done giving up my soul and spirit for this to be the final outcome? I was so hurt and completely shattered. I kept no dignity at all and just burst out crying in Amy's bedroom and couldn't stop. Amy asked me to leave her house for the last time and never go back and I just wanted the ground to swallow me up. I just couldn't stop crying. I begged on my knees for another chance, I pleaded for at least a chance to talk it over, but my lowering, cowering, dribbling husk just made her more angry and determined to get rid of me. I refused to leave, pleading that there was always a way through problems, but Amy wanted me out the house and started to threaten to get her dad to throw me out. She then left me sobbing in her bedroom for an hour while she sat in the living room downstairs with her dad watching television. I eventually got the message and made my way out the house and into the cold dark night.

I started a long and lonely walk back into Chesterfield, I didn't want to get on a bus in the state I was in. I had no energy in me, it was a walk like the walk home from after the Cure concert a few months earlier, knowing that nothing was left for me where I was going back to. Thoughts of suicide filled my head, of disappearing and knowing that once again, no-one would care.

On the road back into Chesterfield I passed a Kingdom Hall. It wasn't the one I used to go to, but it reminded me of my former life, of the many people I used to know and call friends. The church was closed and dark, but I knew the one I used to go to would be open tonight. I missed everyone in the church so much, including all my family.

When I got into Chesterfield my head was no clearer than when I left Amy's home. I was still toying with disappearing, or throwing myself under a passing bus. There was just one other thought and desire in my head, which was to go back to church, crawling and humbled, sad and sorry and begging for forgiveness for my stupidity.

So I kept on walking through Chesterfield town centre and out the other side. My heart had decided on the latter decision to go to the Kingdom Hall, but my head battled with my very soul for control. I knew the questions in my head about the church had never been answered, I knew about the way that I had been treated was cruel, immoral and wrong and I knew that shame and loneliness were cult control techniques to lure me back into the church again. I knew that if I wanted to go back it would mean months of interrogation, judgement and punishment once again as well as still being lonely until I would be accepted back into the congregation as a repentant sinner. I also argued with myself that my "friends" and family would never except me, even with decades of repentant service, because I was soiled goods, imperfect, politically damaged.

None of that mattered though, because my heart was broken and bleeding and I needed solace, care and warmth that I thought I could get from the church. I walked for six miles from Chesterfield to the Kingdom Hall of my former congregation, where all my former friends and family were. I knew I was late, the services always started at seven pm prompt and it was nearly nine by the time I got there.

Everyone stands to sing the last hymn of the day. That tune tears straight into my heart like a dead centred arrow and just makes me lose my balance and I fall onto my seat unable to stop the tears from just bursting out. People see me fall and start looking and staring at me. Someone passes a hymn book into my shaking hands and I start to try and read the writing in the songbook, but there are too many tears in my eyes and I can't focus or stand up.

I actually have no idea what will happen once the song finishes and the last prayer completes. Will anyone talk to me at all, will I be ushered out the door by the elders. I really have no idea.

The song does finish and everything goes quiet except for one voice over the loud speaker system. I struggle to stop sniffling as the tears still keep running uncontrollably making my nose run even more. Someone passes me a tissue and I dab my face, I have no idea who passes it to me as half my vision is blurred and I can't pick my gaze up from the floor because of the weight of shame pressing down hard on my shoulders to the point that I'm nearly in a foetal position on the hard plastic chair.

Finally the prayer over the loudspeakers finishes and I stay in my strange position, watching children's feet scurry through my vision below my bowed head, still weeping. Then I feel a warm caring arm wrap around me, then another and a few pairs of feet fill my vision. I don't want to pick my head up, I feel so ashamed and stupid. The sudden flow of compassion and some kind and warm words just make me start all over again, crying uncontrollably. I have no idea who is hugging me and who is talking to me, the wall of shame is so dense that mixed in with the tears makes a shroud hang over me that I cannot see through.

It takes a few minutes for the tears to slow and my shaking body to settle. As the fit of tears starts to subside another reality begins to kick in. Yes I feel ashamed to be here in the middle of the Kingdom Hall after I have done things completely contrary to what I have been raised and taught to believe, but I also feel such a traitor to myself. I know these people will put on a good show to try and get me back into the congregation, but I also know that unless I throw myself back in completely and without doubt or question, they will all turn their backs on me once again. With such conditions attached to this show of affection, I know that the affection isn't a pure and genuine love, I've always known that and that is why I feel so strongly that I am betraying myself. As much as I miss these people, I don't miss this conditional love.

Reality is kicking in. I know I'm not going to start coming back to church three times a week. I'm not going to try and knock on people's doors and convince strangers of a belief system I'm just not attuned to myself. Once again I feel ashamed and stupid. I'm not going to stoop to the level of these people and lie just to give them what they want. They don't want me, they want a version of me.

I make excuses and start to leave knowing that I won't be going back ever again. This was a lesson harshly learned that my heart and head will always have major battles and neither of them will ever truly be right.

17 DISINTEGRATION

The eighth pill went down without me even noticing. Surely I have done enough now, surely the deed is done. If a single dose is two and a daily dose is four, then the eight I have taken will without doubt kill me.

The music has finished again, the whole album is finished. I'm sure I have time to listen to another shorter album before I rest, before I sleep for the last time. I try and think about what the best last album I will ever listen to should be. Of course there is no dispute really. I put on the Cure's Disintegration album one last time.

I have the picture disc, which is noisy on the turntable. It rumbles quite loudly under the needle until that twinkly star dust sounds just before the first notes crash in. Big padded keyboards and huge drum cymbals introduce the first song and I evaluate where I am.

What I am doing is beautiful for me, it is me. I can only feel so proud of who I am, of being a caring, kind and loving person that values love more than anything else in the world. My heart is full of empathy and caring for everyone in the world and if that isn't good enough for the world, then what a sad world I must live in for the next collection of minutes.

Yes, I can be proud of who I am despite what people do to me and the way they treat me. Somehow I always survive, somehow I always find the strength to pull through and come out the other side. Somehow I prove myself to the world by still being the loving and caring and empathic me. But that is not where I am going now. Now I am on a different path. Forgot this line of reasoning oh treacherous heart, take another pill. Number nine. Yes I am beyond any turnaround.

18 FREEDOM

Ivan's car pulls away and for the first time, I am truly alone.

For the next couple of weeks, this lovely little touring caravan is my home. It feels like such a luxury. I'm dry, warm, I can eat what I want, watch what I want on the TV. I could sleep all day if I wished. It's a long way to ride my bike to work, but then everywhere I've worked has always been that way.

I look out the window and I'm the only touring caravan on the site that is being used and not just here for storage. I can't believe Ivan has done this for me. It's his caravan and he has lent it to me for a couple of weeks until I can find a place more permanent. He's gone out on a limb, I know. He's a Jehovah's Witness and I'm sure there are plenty of people in the congregation, even including my mum, that's telling him he should not be doing this. But he has done it anyway.

I survey my Kingdom. It's only a six birth caravan, but that means I can keep the bed made and still sit in the living area without having to pack everything away every day. I can feel a small amount of chill, so I put the gas fire on. Even on its lowest setting, it's heated the caravan up really nicely.

So what can I do with my new found independence? I have a place of my own, a bit of cash in my pocket and the freedom to be myself.

I throw on my coat and march myself up to the local newsagents just around the corner. I'm so excited I can barely contain myself. I can do something I have never been able to do before, I just need the courage to do it. Once in the local shop, I grab a pack of sausages, a tin of beans then go over to the newspaper stand.

I'm a grown adult. And grown adults buy grown adult magazines all the time, otherwise the makers of said magazines would go bust. This is the outside world now and not the juvenile thinking of the church. I am a man, I have natural needs and I want an adult pornographic magazine.

I firmly stretch up, see a magazine I know the name of and grab if firmly and deliberately. I take the magazine, the sausages and beans to the counter and put the magazine, squarely and firmly in the middle of the counter.

I am not ashamed I am a man with natural needs, damn it.

The man behind the counter doesn't batter an eyelid, asks me for the money and in minutes I'm paid up and I'm out the shop and walking back to my den of debauchery. I cannot believe that I just did that and I walk with my head held high, knowing that I have a wank mag in my plastic bag and I'm quite legally and morally right to have it too.

I love this new found freedom, but it comes at a price. I really am on my own now. No friends, no family, no church to go to, no social events. The only time I will see another human being to talk to will be at work and I just don't fit in with the people there at all. As far as the folk at work are concerned I may as well be from a different planet entirely. My mum looks as though she feels guilty every time I visit her, she probably knows that she is supposed to totally reject me and I can see that conflict within her every time I go there. My relationship with my dad is strained. The reason I am here in this caravan is because my step mum made a final ultimatum to my dad, "it's him or it's me". I still can't work out why, I'm still stupidly naïve and still need to be told when to do things many times because I just don't know myself. I should be wiser at 20 years old. I suppose I'm kind of church wise, I just chose a way out from it. I'm just not world wise at all. At least now, here on my own, my mistakes are my own and will affect just me.

What a strange feeling this is, I feel free, released and able to do anything I put my mind to and yet at the same time this freedom has cost me everything. I have no-one left, no-one. I'm free in my absolute loneliness.

19 AND FINALLY

Robert Smith sings out his heartache to me through the needle on the record. His almost crying voice reflects everything I feel right now, right at this very moment. Nine pills are in my stomach, very likely starting to rip their chemical way through my insides. I can feel no pain, thankfully, but then would I feel anything, after all they are painkillers? I have taken over four times the dosage. There is no doubt in my mind that I have done something irreversible.

The Cure's beautiful dark and warm music just helps to satisfy me that I am in the right place doing the right and the beautiful thing here. It's fully dark outside now. The small electric fire is just about holding the cold away. The measure of just about is emphasized by my warm chest in comparison to my cold back, that is how close the battle for heat is in this shell of a static caravan. I wish I was still in that smaller caravan of Ivan's, that was warm all round.

With each breath I can feel the taste of the electric bar biting the heat into the air and then with another breath the damp tang of coldness from the rest of the air in the cabin.

I look down at the line of pills still lying in front of me. I'm about a quarter of the way through the bottles worth. My mind wonders at a million miles an hour as it always does as to the amount of white pills stretched out before me. Something in my head starts to question why the bottle has so many pills in it. I recall a news item not so long ago about the debate on restricting the number of pills in a bottle to try and stop the very thing I'm doing right now. Many retailers where already taking the recommendations seriously and reducing the bottle sizes. So why then are there still so many pills in this bottle?

I've suddenly got a horrible thought that the nine pills I have taken are nowhere near enough to do the job I expect them to do. The beauty of the last two hours and my honest intention now seem in jeopardy. Am I supposed to finish off all these pills for my plan to work?

I'm so confused. Surely I have gone too far already, surely over a four times dosage is fatal and hopefully not painful.

I've done it now. The thoughts running through my head run like a waterfall, splashing around every corner of my mind with little back turns and eddies. All those memories are all sad, but I came through every single one stronger and more focused. I'm at the lowest I could ever possibly be right now surely. If my death is this very lowest ebb right now, then how can anything that is to come be anywhere near as bad. I'm a feeble, sad and lonely individual, but I have overcome the most horrific turmoil to still be loving, warm and affectionate. I still think more of others than myself and just want to fill the world with a blanket of unconditional love and affection. Surely that will be a loss for humankind? But if it is a loss, even if it's a small sadness in the universe, why is the universe standing by and watching me do this? If god cares where is he right now, why does he not send someone to stop me? Surely god and the universe think I am as unimportant as I do.

The arguments start to sway back and forth in my aching head and heart. I'm so confused now. What was so clear has so easily become so muddied. The voice and music behind me don't help at all and just help to confuse me and spin me in circles.

I am here through my choices. I have got myself here. The universe or god, are not here to rescue me because they didn't put me here. I am here through a culmination of my own decisions and actions. I can blame everyone else in the world, but I am here because of me. I have taken nine pills, no-one else has put them down my throat. I am the sum of my mind and heart. My mind and heart are the result of my journey that I have mapped out for myself.

I am a good and beautiful person. I am on my own because these qualities are rare and my partners in life will be rare to have such qualities as well, it will take time to find any of those other good and beautiful people. I should be proud, not ashamed. The universe needs me, surely.

20 STUPID, STUPID, STUPID

What am I doing? This is all wrong. I have made the wrong decision. I should be fighting not giving up.

Those nine pills will be eating my insides. I suddenly realise the horror of the path I'm well and truly down. If I give in now, there is likely to be hours if not days of huge pain and suffering as my guts are pumped and emptied out and my body is put back together. Do I want to go through that indignity, do I really want to put other people through the sadness of trying to save the life of someone that didn't want it?

I can feel the growing sense of shame. Shame for suddenly changing my mind and for not having the guts to carry on and go through with my beautiful death. I have soiled the dignity and the purity of my actions. My mind is still not made up, but doubt has not just crept in, but leapt in with its whole body and shoved my soul around.

The practicalities of changing my mind stir in my thoughts. Even if I did stop right here, right now, how would I stop this process, where can I go, who can help me?

Shame, I feel so much shame. I'm proud and yet full of sin and shame. I will swallow my pride and stop this, I will stop it now.

I try and think of what I can do now. I've decided to save myself and if it's not too late stop the path of death I'm on. But I'm so very scared. Not just with the shame of admitting to the stupidity of what I was trying to do, but of the fact that I couldn't go through with it and the shame of my family knowing that everything they warned would happen to me has happened. Of course they didn't predict specifics, just warned that I would be on my own if I followed the path I was on. Regardless of my change of mind, the loneliness was an unchanging factor. I have no idea where to turn to, no idea where to go. If I couldn't find anyone that cares in the last hours of my life, then how do I find anyone to steer me away from an oncoming death?
I decide to finish listening to the rest of The Cure's album on the turntable, then I will venture outside into the cold and dark night.

As I listen to the last song on the album, I feel like I'm parting from a friend for the last time ;

"…Never quite managed the words to explain to you
Never quite knew how to make them believable
And now the time has gone
Another time undone
Hopelessly fighting the devil
Futility
Feeling the monster
Climb deeper inside of me

Feeling him gnawing my heart away
Hungrily
I'll never lose this pain
Never dream of you again"

The song finishes, I wipe the tears away from my face and stand up. Time to face my shame.

I feel time is now against me. I need to get to a hospital, but I have no transport. The hospital is several miles away and not on a single bus route. If I start to vomit and pass out on a bus, that would be the worst and most humiliating thing. I would rather carry on my beautiful road to death than go that route.

I slip on my coat and go out into the dark cold night and just start walking. I can't go to my dad's house, they obviously don't care enough and will think I did this all just for attention. The same goes for my mum, she doesn't care either and she will only see my suicide attempt as sinful. I have a very small telephone book in my pocket. In it are just a handful of telephone numbers. By the time I get to a telephone box, I'm wondering if there is anyone I can call that will help. My uncle is a wonderful person, but doesn't deal with other people's emotions very well. My former religious mentor Rob, surely he would help?

I ring his number from my book and the telephone just rings and rings. I can feel my stomach gurgling. Is that the pills, or am I just over sensing everything in my panic? Rob's telephone just will not pick up. I frantically go through my small phone book again. There really is nobody, I'm going to die anyway, even though I've changed my mind.

There's one telephone number left in the book. It belongs to Ivan the kind guy that lent me his touring caravan for two weeks a couple of months ago and who found this static caravan for me to rent. I didn't want to involve him, I'm not his problem and he had gone far and above just basic kindness already in what he had done for me.

I frantically tried to think of anyone else that could help me. I couldn't believe my situation. I used to belong to a congregation of over a hundred people, all of whom I knew intimately, as well as an extremely large family on my mums side of aunts, uncles, great uncles, cousins, 2nd cousins and yet here I was on the very edge of death itself with no-one to answer my call for help. I would help anyone and everyone, so why was the world and the inner world of my former religion so loveless?

With no-where else to go I nervously call Ivan's telephone number. When he picks up the phone and answers it takes me by surprise and I don't know what to say. I mumble and start crying and try and tell him that I've taken a load of pills and don't know what to do now I've changed my mind. Ivan calmly tells me to go home and he will come and pick me up. I ask him not to ever tell my mum, as I know that would likely be his first reaction and he promises to me that he will keep it all quiet.

I put the phone down and walk back to the caravan. I barely get back when Ivan arrives in his car and asks me how many pills I've taken. For the first time when I tell him I have taken nine paracetamols, I wonder if that actually is a lot or not. It suddenly dawns on me that if it's not a lot then I have even more to be ashamed of. Suddenly that thought then makes me wonder how stupid I'm going to look if nine is a small number. Then that thought just cascades into a feeling of being an absolute idiot that is just so stupid he doesn't even know how to kill himself properly.

My brain will just not shut up. I'm arguing with myself again that perhaps I should try again properly and do it properly. I feel so ashamed.

Ivan puts me in his car along with a few quickly gathered clothes and he drives me just a couple of miles away to his house. On the journey I ask Ivan again that he doesn't tell my mum about this whole affair and again he gives me his word. Ivan doesn't ask any questions, doesn't probe and just tells me to relax as he and his wife Sarah are going to take care of me.

When we get to Ivan's house, Ivan asks me again how many pills I've taken and makes me a cup of tea and wraps me in a duvet. While supping my tea in the kitchen, I can hear Sarah on the phone to the hospital in the distant room telling the nurses how many pills I've taken and what they are. When Sarah comes back in the room and tells Ivan and myself that I don't need to go into the hospital and just drink plenty of water, I realise with a huge amount of shock and embarrassment, that nine pills is nowhere near enough to even warrant a hospital visit.

I feel so stupid and so ashamed. What an idiot I am. I am relieved that I don't have to go to hospital, that I don't have to have my stomach violently pumped empty of pills and of course relieved that I'm not actually going to die after all, now that I've decided to live.

Both Sarah and Ivan are both so wonderfully sweet. Neither of them ask, nor interrogate me as to why I tried to commit suicide, although I'm also now getting a sense that they might think I had no serious intention of doing so. I really didn't want to get into any questioning, I just want to be safe. Ivan forces me to drink a whole pint of water in front of him, then Sarah gets the spare bedroom ready for me and puts two more pint glasses of water next to the bed. I'm then sent straight to bed with instruction to drink the water and sleep and not worry about getting up in the morning.

Strangely, I slept so soundly and clear of mind.

21 EPILOGUE

That crazy night was twenty seven years ago. It took nearly 15 years to work out that I had been conned by a cult and that my soul wasn't actually damned for an eternity. Instead I'm now looking at my family, still stuck inside the church with no foreseeable way out and they still think that I'm bad and should not be associated with.

I don't feel bitter, in fact I feel so very sorry for them because they cannot see what I see. Their society is crumbling, worldwide huge reports of child sex abuses and cover ups by the organisation are ripping the church into pieces and yet those still stuck in it don't see any of it.

An Australian Royal commission blamed the Jehovah's Witnesses organisation for systematically covering up child sex abuse on an unprecedented scale. The main headquarters in New York are paying out millions in compensation to abuse victims around the world, and yet their own followers are blind to it all happening under their noses.

I feel protective over those still stuck inside the "Truth"

as they call it. Like a drunk or drug taker, they just cannot see what they are mixed up in and through intense fear, cannot get out of it as they will lose everything they have ever known.

I'm now happily married with a wonderful kind and warm loving partner, have a lovely dog and a mortgage.

There has been so much of the last twenty years that I would have missed out on if that night would have gone as originally planned. There have been some awful things happen as they always do in life. But what matters is how you deal with those things and come through stronger and better for it. I decided never to have children because I could never think of putting another human being through what I have been through.

In my opinion, we become the sum of our choices. You cannot change the decisions you have made, but those decisions can better inform your future ones.

I have loved, many times. I have made music, performed it live and released music, directed a couple of music videos, created artworks, seen some amazing places around the world and met some amazing people and shared some interesting philosophies. I've worked and lived on the bread line and worked and been comfortable. I have had some rich experiences since that dark night many years ago. If I could live my life again from the beginning I would choose not to, but I have this life and I intend to live it with love. My only real heartache is seeing how the majority of people in the world just cannot see how beautiful everything could be if we just loved each other. There is just hate, anger and a dark evil in all places, hearts and gatherings, including the Jehovah's Witnesses organisation as much as anywhere else.

If you ever find yourself sitting in front of a row of white pills, please just take a moment. We could fill the world with love, instead of leaving it cold.

ABOUT THE AUTHOR

Jonny Halfhead started his public artistry as a keyboard player in a Gothic Rock band in the nineties. His life has been spent writing and recording music, creating works of art, performing on stage and writing fiction and non-fiction. Born into and living in a religious cult for twenty years has shaped his personality in an almost unique way as a person of love, empathy and compassion and uses his dark artistry as a means of therapy.

Printed in Great Britain
by Amazon